FEATHER AND BONE

MELISSA WRIGHT

THE FREY SAGA

FEATHER *and* BONE

MELISSA WRIGHT

FEATHER
and BONE

FEATHER

FREY

I HAD BROUGHT EACH OF MY SEVEN HOME FROM BATTLE, ALIVE and nearly intact, but it had not been without cost. The changeling Pitt was gone. We had destroyed him before he was able to carry out the worst of his plans, to unleash a darkness capable of destroying elves and fey alike. But I had made a deal with the fey.

The first order of business once we'd returned from Hollow Forest was to place a new boundary against the fey. It wasn't meant as a replacement for the one bordering fey lands but to be a barrier closer to our home—one to surround the castle. There would be no more nobbling of my guard to have them hauled across the kingdom.

No one would touch Ruby again.

"The eastern barrier has been completed," Rhys reported, his cropped silver hair and guard-issue attire in perfect order. "Two more days, and the northern one will be done as well."

I nodded. "And what of the manuscript? Have you had any luck deciphering its symbols?" I hoped from the etchings on the cover and the details of energy transfer inside that it might give us some clue to aid in our quest.

"I'm afraid we have not." He gestured toward his brother. Rider slid a document forward on the long wooden planks of the library table. "We've found several similar etchings on one of Vita's scrolls. We suggest submitting them to Junnie, as they appear to be related to her line and the light elves."

Anvil stood quietly opposite me, his arms crossed over his wide chest. There was something that felt dangerous about meddling in magics we did not understand. But I didn't suppose there was much we could do to stop it.

It was bad, and our prospects had only seemed worse the longer I'd had to think about it. I pushed down the fear of revealing my plan, because not doing so would risk too much beyond our own lives. "I believe we have more information than we realized."

My Seven, at least those who were present, stared back at me. Steed had fared well in the attack on the castle, and Anvil, Rhys, and Rider had come home from fey lands mostly unscathed. Chevelle stood beside me, but even if he was too stubborn to admit it, he needed time to heal from the battle in Hollow Forest. I swallowed hard at the memory, at the image of Ruby consumed by flame. She rested in her rooms, and Liana was tending to her wounds, which would take longer to knit back together. Grey supervised Liana's care of Ruby. His wounds were more the visible sort, and together—I hoped—he and Ruby would soon be healed.

I sat straighter, drawing in a steadying breath. "After the attack on Veil's home, Junnie confessed her concerns regarding Isa. The girl apparently has a talent with the humans not because of her heritage or the crossing of bloodlines."

My guard waited in stillness, the consistent flicker of firelight in the sconces along the wall the only movement in the room.

"Isa lives because Asher used spellcasting on her human mother while the child was still in her womb. It is how she was brought to term." This much they may have known.

My guard had tracked down the other of Asher's children, the ones who had not been as lucky. They had found broken bodies destroyed by magic. It was the reason that so many disdained the crossing of the bloodlines. That kind of crossing didn't work. It was wrong—not due to some simple distaste for another's kind, but because what resulted was nothing but the deaths of the mothers who attempted it and the deaths of their children.

"But that was not the only casting he performed. It seems Isa's ability, her control over the humans, manifested due to Asher's spellwork."

I let them sit with that, gave them time to take it in. It was no small thing. Each had been present when I had killed Asher, when I'd forced the human girl he'd been using as a broodmare to drive a knife through his ribs. They had heard Asher's words, the spell he had cast with his dying breath.

My forebear had given me the power he'd gained from his ancestors, the power he'd wrought with darkness and spells. It writhed inside of me even as I sat as Lord of the North. It was too much for one body to wield, and I was not Asher. I was only his half-human heir.

"And now," I continued, "Isa is safely away from Council and those who might do her harm at the revelation, but what Asher has brought upon us is not so easily undone. Junnie does not have the answers the fey want, and neither do we, but only two halfbloods survive. Only two of us live and breathe."

Anvil had always understood the significance of our being

halfbreeds, and I suspected it was something Steed had considered of Ruby, but the brothers—born in a faraway land and only recently learning of these treacheries and the fey—seemed to recognize the importance of that connection right away.

I restlessly tapped a finger on the hilt of my sword. "Ruby's mother had apparently detailed the process in her diary, but that is gone, traded to Liana in exchange for Chevelle."

He was steady beside me, and I didn't look at him when I spoke, but I was still annoyed that he'd bargained his own life away to get me out of my bonds.

"Ruby has assured me that anything of import was long ago removed from its pages. That means only one of us has the secret to the casting that allowed Ruby to live." Ruby and Ruby alone had memorized the passages her mother had written then destroyed them so no one else could see. "We may be able to use her knowledge to understand how the fey were planning to implement it, how to untie those bonds to the base energy beneath fey lands." *Once she is well enough to tell us, anyway.*

I cleared my throat. "Unfortunately, none of us knows the method Asher used to impart unto Isa the ability she has. No one but the changeling fey."

My guard let out a collective breath. The changelings had let loose a darkness that was eating away at the base magic—the very lifeblood of the fey—and none of us knew how to stop it. It was our most pressing problem.

"And what do we know of the spellcaster?" Rider asked, his expression solemn.

I glanced at Chevelle. He looked a little pale, but I assumed that was owing to the pain in his side. He stepped forward. "We have sent out scouts, and the fey have set a bounty, but no dependable leads have come to any of us yet." He took a shallow breath. "The caster made an attempt on a Council head's life. Junnie has set a vow to repay the debt."

Rhys shifted. "Has she healed from the attack?"

Chevelle nodded. "Word is that she's making arrangements to gather more trackers now."

Steed threw Chevelle a sharp look. "The call?"

"Yes. She's reinstituted the calling, but service is voluntary." His tone seemed to imply "for now."

None of us had much taste for the calling, a term of servitude put in place by the previous Council heads. Junnie had to take a firm hand in her new role as head of the light elves, but the fact that she'd resorted to falling back on old traditions didn't bode well for any of us.

"And what of our own?" I asked. "What news from the rogues and Camber, now that we've traipsed once again onto fey lands and into a plaguing mess?"

Anvil's expression was level.

"Tell me," I said, thinking that it couldn't be any worse than the bargain I'd made with a fey lord.

Anvil uncrossed his arms only to tuck his thumbs into his sword belt. "Your mother was a driving force in the events that brought about the massacre of the North, even if it was Council who cut down our people. Her sister burned and razed the villages and Council temples of the South. Between the two, they've done more damage than any fey war has ever managed."

I stared at him flatly.

He shrugged one shoulder. "It certainly has not helped foster the idea that halfbloods should be allowed to live."

Let alone rule. "Will there be any open challenges to my rule?" I asked.

The corner of his mouth drew down, leveled out. "Not if this is resolved before the fey cross onto our lands."

I nodded. "Then we will see that it is done."

~

THE MEETING ADJOURNED, Anvil and Steed took up a conversation about the goings-on in Camber while Rhys and Rider went back to their research of the fey energy. I turned to Chevelle. His expression told me he understood that I meant to ask him to rest in our rooms but that he had duties of his own—a castle to run and a guard to oversee. I frowned. It was not the first conversation of the sort we'd had. "Walk with me, then?"

He nodded, standing slowly before following me out. In the long corridor outside the study, our steps were measured.

"This is not the first mistake I've made."

He kept his gaze forward, his tone steady. "There will always be time to second-guess your actions. What counts is that you make decisions and take action when it needs taking. No one can fault you for that."

"I can. And I do." I ran a hand over my face. "I've put everything at risk, time and again." I'd done worse—I'd made a deal that was terrifying in its open-endedness with a fey lord. All to save Ruby.

We walked past ornate doorways, the crest of my line carved into metal plates over dark wood and woven into scenes on the tapestries. No one was left of Asher's line but Isa and me. "Maybe they're right," I said. "Maybe I have no business taking his throne."

Chevelle's jaw went tight, his gaze snapping to mine. "It was never *his* throne. He stole it by deceit and trickery by making deals with the fey."

My hand went up to gesture vaguely at his words, because I'd just made a similar deal.

He shook his head. "It is not the same, and you know it. There was nothing honorable about his rule." Chevelle's tone seemed to add that there was nothing honorable about the man, either, but Asher was gone, and my second would not speak ill of him merely for sport.

"I don't know what I'm doing. I can barely keep my feet on the stone, let alone secure the entire kingdom." I ran a palm over the leather at my hip, which was uncomfortably bare of staff or sword. "The right thing to do was let Ruby go. Let the fey play their games and strike them only when we were sure, when we had the upper hand and good standing."

Chevelle glanced at me.

"I was weak," I told him. "I was weak then, and I will be weak again the moment I'm tested. For any of you."

The words sounded too much like Asher's long-ago warnings against my relationship with Chevelle, and he turned, taking my arm and drawing me to a stop beneath a pair of ornate metal sconces. "Caring about your people, your guard, is not a weakness. It is what makes you worthy to rule."

I cast my eyes down, and he tightened his grip, the act bringing my gaze back to his.

"The lack of those very traits is what caused Asher to risk us all. He was the catalyst for this mess, not you."

I sighed, unconvinced.

Chevelle drew me closer, his words a vow. "There is no other I would trust with untangling our land from the foul mire we are in. You are lord because you have earned it with your blood, your honor, your very life. I follow you—we all follow you—because you are the rightful lord. We trust in you. You are worthy."

My throat went dry at the conviction in his tone. "Even if I am…"

He didn't argue further, because I was right: there was no

guarantee that anyone, worthy or not, could stand against the forces at play, let alone the strange darkness corrupting the fey energy. "You should eat something," he finally said.

I gave him a look. "Are you implying I'm ill-tempered when I'm hungry?"

The corner of his mouth quirked, but he shook his head. "I wouldn't dare."

VEIL

Veil sat reclined in a vine-woven chair, its seat padded with thick palm-blossom bedding and scattered with pillows. He stared unspeaking at the changeling fey seated across from him, but she only watched as two of Veil's attendants cleaned his skin with oils. He was shirtless, weaponless, and only partially healed, but everyone present understood that he was strong enough to kill her on a whim.

His new attendant, Kel, brushed Veil's amber wing, and Liana's eyes roamed over Kel's fingers as if counting the bones beneath his flesh. Veil did not want Liana there. He did not want any of them there, but his other home had been destroyed. The changeling Pitt and his vile spellcasters had destroyed the showplace where Veil had hosted guests. So he sat with his personal guard and the changeling Liana in one of the last secure spaces that had been unknown to his previous guard, the heliotrope warriors who had betrayed him.

Liana's lips tilted into a grin. "You look good with a solid brood on. It fits you well."

Veil rolled his eyes heavenward, but his gaze only met the

dark wood of a tightly braided canopy. It was like being trapped in a cave, and there was nothing he could think of worse than being constrained by stone and earth.

Cyren, the second of only two attendants Veil had chosen when the others had been removed from their posts, moved to clean Veil's feet, but the fey lord gestured the pair away. The act felt too intimate with the changeling fey watching. Her black eyes made everything feel too near, too *seen*.

The fey gave Liana a glance as they walked from Veil's private room. Her answering smile was predatory. "They are quite lovely," she purred as she stood, "though I can't say their talents will be as useful as their predecessors'."

His wing twitched at the reminder, and Liana's smile went soft. "There, now," she said, "let me have a look at you."

Liana peeled back a layer of the leaves and bandages covering Veil's arm, her dark eyes examining the wound as her careful fingers cleared away the ointments and tonic. She'd had to leave it longer than she'd wanted, she'd explained, because her bargains bound her first to the elven lord and her Seven.

Veil had not believed Liana in the least, because the changelings always had motives beyond their word, but he had not pressed her. "And how fares the halfling who survived the fires of Hollow Forest?"

Liana's brow tilted, but she kept to her work. "She will live, should she not tempt the fates again." She tossed a bit of frond and stitching over her shoulder then reached into the pouch at her waist for a thin vial. "She wakes occasionally, ranting of winged horses and flying elves." Liana's gaze brushed Veil's.

He did not respond.

She let out a huff of air that might have been a laugh, had she bothered to spell it to life.

"And what of you?" he asked. "Do you plan to tell me how you manage to draw on the base energy outside of fey lands?"

Her fingers stilled, but only for a heartbeat. There was no other indication she'd even heard him speak.

"As I suspected." Veil glanced at the small table beside his reclined chair, which held the dark-red wine she'd laced with something for the pain. The decanter was still as full as when she'd left it. He would not trust anyone enough to fall into a state of distrait or into anything other than vigilance and allow himself to be caught. Not again.

Liana tugged at his wound, and Veil's finger twitched. "I cannot stay long," she told him. "They will know where I've been. They have set a full guard on me and have the most vexing collection of sentries dropping in on me throughout the day."

"Where do they think you are now?"

"Resting." She met his gaze, the orange glow of the light flickering against depthless black in her eyes. "But that won't last long. They're constructing a barrier to keep out all fey."

Veil sat up. It pulled his wound. His skin felt of the burn of ice, and Liana pushed him back down.

"Be still," she warned. "We will work out a means around it. Even if it costs a bit of work."

Veil sighed, closing his eyes as the cool flesh of Liana's fingertips grazed his skin. There was something unsettling, so unlike the other fey, about the changeling. He'd yet to distinguish what it was, exactly, and it was driving him to distraction.

A sharp scent cut through his ruminations, and he opened his eyes to find she'd bitten into a caddlefruit. She held half between her fingers, pulling the other half free to rub over the edge of the wound. The pulp was deep red, dark, and pungent. He watched the color that stained her lips give light to her cheeks, trailing briefly toward the line of her jaw. It spread, flushing her skin as it crossed her neck and shoulders, dipping into the thin silks of her clothes. He wondered if she was toying with him. He wondered why he was bothering to look.

When his gaze met hers, she blinked then patted the new bandages into place. "Leave these on for two moons and try not to get stabbed again by a poison blade."

He let her see his distaste for the quip.

She smirked. "Any news of the spellcasters?"

"They've gone into hiding. I expect them only to regroup when they may strike again."

She crossed her slender arms, her flesh still blushed with the color of ripened fruit. He could still smell it filling the room, too, and he had to make his gaze stay on her dark eyes. She didn't seem to notice. "They've no reason to hurry, I suppose. The longer they wait, the more desperate your people become."

"*My* people," he echoed.

One of her shoulders shifted in something of a shrug as she uncrossed her arms. "The fey."

He narrowed his gaze on her.

"I have to go. Bargains with the elven court and all that." Liana gestured teasingly before drawing another vial out of her pouch. "Something for the pain," she said, glancing pointedly at the full decanter of wine. "This is to be inhaled, and it will not put you to sleep."

He took it from her, the glass cool in his hand. Veil inclined his head toward her in thanks, and she smiled in return.

"I will send word as soon as I've any to send," she said.

With the promise, she turned and walked from the room. Veil stared after her, holding the vial and smelling the bitter tang of her ministrations. He had trusted his heliotropes only because if one had meant to betray him, the other would have read it from her mind. His false sense of safety had been rooted in the idea that he could not be betrayed by both. He wouldn't make the same mistake again. He would not leave himself open to the whim of fate.

He laid the vial on the table beside the wine then sat up to stretch his arm and test the strength of his connection to the base energy. Veil was a fey lord. Veil could wield power enough to change the seasons.

He would not be brought down by a changeling and a handful of spellcasting fey.

RUBY

RUBY WRITHED IN HER DREAMS, TRAPPED BY CLAWING HANDS and rivers of darkness. They pulled at her, wanting to drown her. Everything smelled of violet and amaranth, of deep forest spices and oil of myrrh. She knew she was sleeping and understood that those scents meant she'd been put under by the changeling fey. Not the changeling who had tied her to the spellwork, but the other, Liana, who had dragged her from the darkness with the fey lord, Veil.

Ruby couldn't think about any of that, though. She could only fight to stay afloat, to keep above that tide of shadows.

Everything that had happened, all that had befallen her and those she cared about, was her fault. She had to get out and let them know.

She felt the warmth of Grey's touch, his hand in hers a constant presence. She was numb to many things, but she could feel the bumps and ridges of his scars, reminders of another fire and of the power she was up against.

She needed to wake up. She needed to be free of the flames that were not hers.

She had to escape before they were all out of time.

ISA

ISA STARED DOWN AT THE GRAY BODY HER MEN HAD ENCASED IN broad leaves and twined within a net. They had dragged it over the border after finding it near fey lands, so it was her problem to deal with.

She glanced up at Taryn. The problem wasn't going away. They'd spotted three more bodies, all of which had disappeared into the depths of the fey forest in the last month. It meant someone on fey lands knew what was happening. It meant word would get back. "I'll send a missive to Junnie," Isa said. She would have to word it carefully and keep it brief enough to suspend suspicion.

Isa's sentries already had to keep back other threats. The humans in her care were highly superstitious and had started crafting legends for the darkness that bordered their lands.

They didn't know it was the fey who feared them. They didn't realize how much danger they were truly in. The fey would sooner see the entirety of the humans dead than face the risk they posed.

"Make haste," Isa told Taryn. "Gather a small contingent.

We'll deliver this body to the Lord of the North, and her people can take responsibility."

Freya was already tied to the fey lord in bargain, and she had taken on the debt of the humans and the deadening of the base magic. The deaths would be hers to deal with.

Junnie could attend by her own choice—Isa could give her that option and knew that Junnie would. But Junnie need not be beholden to any fey, let alone their lord, and Isa could manage that much for her.

5

FREY

I SAT OVER A BOOK OF LEGENDS FROM THE ICE LANDS, A GIFT from Rhys that had taken him a while to hunt down. I'd lost track of the words on the page hours before, and instead slipped away into thoughts of magic and long-ago spells. I had been taught by a master of those skills, by a being so powerful that none could challenge his rule. He had employed his guard to train me, as well, and between those lessons and what I had learned by watching, I knew enough to hang on to my throne. But Asher had not been overthrown by a single being. He had been taken from power long before his human prize drove a blade into his chest.

He had been removed by Council and those who opposed him. He had been knocked from his seemingly stable ground by his own daughter. In truth, he'd been defeated by his own actions and his desire for power.

I closed the cover of the book, tracing a finger over the fine silver lines embossed into darkened leather. Power surrounded me, swimming through me so forcefully that I could barely keep it under control some days. But it was getting easier. I had managed to keep my temper mostly in check, and the constant presence of Chevelle and my Seven had reminded me why it was so important to do so.

What Asher had spelled inside of me with his dying breath was a dark and dangerous thing. It was mine, no matter how much it felt like it could overwhelm me, and it was tied to the energy I'd been born with as his heir. That didn't mean I knew how it worked.

The spellcasting he'd performed then was likely similar to the work he'd attempted on his child Isa, and yet, I could not be sure precisely how he'd done it. I recalled a tale from Ruby of how magic—the energy itself—could potentially be transferred upon ending a life. It had seemed like such a myth at the time, because it had come when I'd been bound and had only the memories of my time with the light elves.

The light elves did not abide by the darkness that was Asher's magic, and they'd certainly not wanted me to recall any part of it.

And because Ruby lay healing, lost somewhere to the fires of Hollow Forest, I could not ask her again about the tale she'd evidently wanted me to know. I could not say how long she'd been aware the fey were coming, how long she'd had ideas of Asher's plans. I could only wait for her to recover and hope she had answers she was willing to give.

I sighed and glanced at the figure who'd been shadowing the doorway. "You do not have to watch me every moment. The worst of it is over. The boundaries are almost completed."

I could hear the disagreement in my guard's silence. There was a spellcaster out there, someone who had helped the changeling Pitt and who wanted to break free of the fey lands and the energy that held them there.

"I read more of the water dragons of Rhys's and Rider's homeland," I told the figure, "and how the creatures came onto land to devour all the energy they could find once the drought had eaten up their own." The legends of the ice lands were far different than those of the fey. Fey tales were cautionary things, in which someone—or someones—often died in their attempt to reach more power. The legends in my new book, though, were heroic tales of conquering beasts and triumph for the elves.

They reeked of falsehoods. The fey were prone to exaggeration, but there were far more truths in their legends of death and destruction than in those where all worked toward the greater good. Rhys and Rider had left their home as their own lives were at risk, threatened by a king and the superstition of their people. The wolves had brought the brothers to us to aid in our dilemma, and I had been grateful for it for as long as I had known them.

How or why the wolves had traveled all the way to the ice lands, though, remained to be seen.

"It would be nice to find the connection," I muttered, tossing aside another scroll.

"And what if none of it is connected?" Steed asked quietly.

"Have you been told to leave me be?" I asked. "To lurk in the shadows?"

He laughed, leaning against the doorway on an elbow. "Only to give you your space."

I scoffed. "As much space as is between the door and this desk, it seems."

Steed inclined his head, strolling into the room to take a seat opposite me. "As long as I need not give you enough space to run into trouble."

"Hmm."

"Indeed." He shrugged. It wasn't his decision, after all.

I narrowed my gaze on him. "That aside, I'm surprised you of all people would suggest there's no connection."

Steed leaned forward to place his elbows on his knees. "Oh, I'm sure there are at least a few connections. A web of them, no doubt. But maybe not *all* of it is connected." He rolled a thumb over the knuckle of his first finger, not quite making a fist. "There are pieces missing, obviously. Pieces are gone, or the fey wouldn't need us." He waved toward me. "You, anyway."

Ruby and me. The halflings. Spelled into life. "I sometimes wonder what this will cost us," I said, "and what all this will mean for the lot of us."

His expression was level as he looked back at me. "Whatever the cost, these deeds would have been done with or without us." His words said something deeper than just that. They held the tone of loyalty, as if Steed, too, felt I was worthy of my post, as if he'd rather it was me there than anyone else.

I drew a deep breath. I wished I had his confidence. "So where do we look for those missing pieces?"

He tapped the thumb against a knuckle. "And what of those dragons, the ones who subsist on an energy beneath the land?"

I leaned toward him, intrigued.

"Were there not dragons in the fey lands? Not so long ago…" Steed said.

I didn't see the connection he was trying to make. "They didn't leave because of the base energy. They were driven away by the fey, during the chaos of the war."

Steed lifted one brow, his gaze steady.

"You think the fey chased them off to secure more power? Because…" I shook my head. "No, they'd only feed the base energy if they were killed. If that many dragons left, they would take their energy along. It would never be returned to the source."

"And they would never again feed from the source. It would be an even trade."

I sat back in my chair, unconvinced. "I've never heard even an inkling of this tale."

Steed smiled. "Have you listened to none of my sister's stories? The fey only make legends of the tales they want told. Should a prize warrant it, they can keep their deeds a secret as long as any of the rest of us."

"I doubt that."

He chuckled. "Well, longer than their reputations for it, at least."

I tried to think of the last time I'd seen a dragon. When I was a child, maybe I saw the shadow of one far over the eastern plains. "Where are they now, then, if they cannot draw from the base energy—if that is even how the dragons live?"

"I used to hear word about them on my trades. The imps were terrified of the creatures and were constantly warning each other off any direction where one might have been seen. But I'm not certain they would need to gather that energy as often as the fey. They certainly aren't using it up as swiftly."

I pressed my lips together, thinking of Liana and the way she seemed to need access far less than the normal fey. I blew out a breath. "This isn't really clearing up the way all of it connects for me."

Steed smiled. "Oh, it was never meant to. I was only giving you a break." He glanced at the doorway then stood, turning his head to give me a hidden wink as he made his way past the desk. "She's all yours," he called over his shoulder.

I swallowed a snort of laughter, giving Chevelle a moment to clear the irritation off his face before I turned to him. "And how fares the business of the castle?" I asked.

He gave me a level look.

"That good?"

"The rogues have been restless. Nothing out of the ordinary." He shifted his weight.

I frowned at him. "Don't make me order you to take rest."

He frowned back at me. He had to know I would.

"What's left?" I asked. "I'll take some of the burden from you."

Chevelle shook his head. "It's under control."

I slid my chair back to stand. "Fine. Then I'll be in our rooms, waiting on you." I gave him a honeyed smile as he appeared to bite back what was probably a warning that I should be watched.

◈

As I WALKED down the cool stone corridor to our rooms, I thought of what Steed had said about the dragons. I'd never considered that the fey could have driven them from their lands for any reason other than the reserve of power. There were still a few about, but not near the castle, and certainly not near anything fey. I pushed open the heavy plank door to the room, annoyed at the tingle of spellcasting that lingered against my palm despite my having warned Chevelle to leave it be. My guard would protect me. The barriers would hold. I did not need that darkness so near where we slept.

I sighed, closing the door behind me and dropping my sword belt onto the long table against the wall. With a thought, I flared the candles in the room to life, and I had to focus to steady the magic to an even flow. I tossed down my knives and loosened the straps of my leather chest plate, decorative armor fit more for the formality of a lord's duty than for battle. I crossed toward the bed, intending to stretch out and close my eyes to find my birds, but a whisper of sound—the scratch of leather on stone—cut me short.

It was the sound of a boot sole sliding across the floor.

I spun, palms thrown forward to make my attack, and found the form of a golden idol, the fey lord. I did not drop my hands. "What are you doing here?" I hissed.

He remained leaning casually against the wall of my room, one leg crossed over the other as he examined a small carved gem. I recognized it as a brooch from my own box of jewels. He tossed it aside. It landed near a dish on a side table, beside a goblet, from which he'd apparently been drinking our wine. Several other gems lay scattered over the table, but one was noticeably missing. "I'm here to remind you of our bargain," he said smoothly.

My palms itched to strike him, but I held the power still.

His eyes bored into mine. "Did you think I would not have received word of your *fey* barriers? That you were trying to keep me out?"

"I care not about your gossip and even less about your rules. This is the second time you've broken into my personal rooms, and I have no intention of letting it pass."

The tilt to the corner of his mouth said I was mistaken about it only being the second time, and my stomach dipped at the idea. He straightened, uncrossing his ankles to stand tall, wings tucked neatly against his back. Veil towered over me, but I was not afraid of him, not on our own soil.

"We have an agreement." His voice was low, a warning that ignored my own threat. "Your vow is sealed, and your promise is mine." His amber eyes were warm despite the shadows crossing the room. In them was a promise of his own. "Whatever it takes."

The words sent a chill over my skin. It wasn't fear. It was the trade, a bargain made and sworn. I'd agreed to help him stop the darkness poisoning his lands, whatever it took. There was no backing out. I glared at Veil. "My vow does not excuse

MELISSA WRIGHT

you from the rule of law. And no matter our agreement, I will strike you down, should you ever step foot inside my rooms again."

He moved closer, training his gaze on mine. "And here I was, hoping you'd be amenable to a discussion."

"We will meet on neutral ground. Send a messenger, and my guard and I will treat with you at the border."

"Your *guard*," he hissed, "was not part of the bargain. You, dear Freya, are my prize."

Fire licked at my fingertips, wanting to tear free of me and burn him to the ground. "I am no one's prize."

His brow shifted, but he did not speak the thoughts that seemed to cross his mind. He drew a long-suffering sigh. "I no more want to be here than you desire me to be. But it seems you've forgotten the stakes."

"I am well aware."

He glanced at the window, shifting casually, as if he was not purposefully moving nearer to the heat of my outthrust palms. "Asher betrayed his vow, broke the terms of his bargain with the fey."

I let my glare remind him I was not Asher. Asher was dead.

He waved a hand vaguely over his shoulder, eying the drapes drawn back at the head of the bed. His gaze shot back to mine. "I will not be betrayed."

His promise seemed to include "again," and I bit back my words. I would not argue my honor with a plaguing fey.

"Your word is binding, and as fey lord, should I be *stricken down*, as you so callously put it, your bargain will still be binding to my people and to whomever takes my place."

The heat in my palms went cold. He thought I would let them die, and apparently, that someone might have a chance to actually destroy him. "You've found the spellcaster?"

26

He frowned, shifting another step closer. "No. They've hidden themselves well."

"They," I echoed.

His gaze returned to mine, allowing me to see the truth in it.

I felt myself deflate. This was bad. I ran a hand over my face. As much as I wanted to punish Veil for the trespass, for the time being, we shared an enemy who was a danger to far more than either of us.

There was a sound at the door, and I turned to look, startled for a moment at the expression that came over Chevelle's face. And then I remembered I was standing with an intruder of the worst possible sort.

Chevelle was moving before I had a chance to get a command out, though I wasn't certain even what it would be. I'd only just threatened Veil, myself. Chevelle slammed into Veil just as the fey lord raised his palms, and the two went flying toward the outer wall in a riotous spin. Veil's wings went wide, blocking Chevelle's strike, and the fey lord pressed hands against my Second's skin. Chevelle was in his guard attire, which left only half his neck and the flesh of his face exposed, but Veil had managed decent contact, anyway. I was fairly certain they would not actually kill one another.

"I wouldn't," I cautioned, but they were beyond listening to me. The heat of Veil's power swam through the room, and Chevelle's expression went hard. His hand shifted between them, his mouth moving in a whisper of ancient words, and then darkness clouded the space.

"Enough!" I shot out.

The commotion had apparently alerted the guards at the end of the corridor, because footfalls echoed down the hall. "Wonderful," I muttered. "We've an audience now."

When two guards burst through the half-opened door, I

waved them away. Then, because they'd seen a cloud of smoke and writhing forms, I had to order them back with a command. They waited out of sight in the hallway, weapons drawn and still.

"Enough," I said again, but the forms inside the darkened cloud had also stilled. The smoke dissipated, and Chevelle stepped back, straightening his breastplate and the neck of his shirt. A claw mark ran from the base of his ear into his collar, and he had a bit of something orange smudged across his cheek. He kept his gaze on Veil, who seemed unable to free himself from the blackened vines crawling up the thighs of his pants.

I stepped forward, staring. My voice was a whisper. "What did you do?"

Chevelle didn't answer. Clearly, it was spellcasting, and clearly, he felt justified in tying a fey lord to the stones of our bedroom floor.

I couldn't say I disagreed.

I crossed my arms, glancing from the vines to Veil's face. I had to swallow a hiccup of hysterical laughter. I cleared my throat.

"Your vow you will never again trespass," I said.

Veil stared at me, plainly both incredulous and incensed.

I lifted one shoulder in a shrug. "He's done no wrong. You are in his bedroom, after all, and have trespassed against his lord." I sighed. "To be honest, his duty as my Second would really put this into his hands. I suppose I should just let him decide your fate."

Veil's look turned to betrayal. I let him see the quirk to the corner of my mouth. He went pale. It was not a good color on him. "I vow to never again enter this room," he said coldly.

"Oddly specific, wouldn't you say?"

Veil's mouth was a hard line. He would never agree to vow

that he wouldn't trespass at all, as it would be too difficult for him to uphold. "Without permission," he added, which seemed to imply something Chevelle probably would not like. I didn't glance at my Second to confirm.

"And to cause Chevelle no harm," I said.

Veil glared sidelong at me.

I uncrossed my arms to lay a hand on my hip where my sword might have rested, had I not foolishly tossed it away before checking the room. "Surely, you do not believe I will trust you not to repay this without a vow."

"I stand here, bound. This is hardly a fair bargain."

"You speak as if you've never trapped a lord into a bargain. Say it."

His glare narrowed. "I vow to not repay him this offense."

"Do we still have a dungeon?" My words were for Chevelle, but I kept my gaze on Veil.

"Only the pit," he said from beside me. "But I think it will do." Chevelle's answer was quiet but smooth. He was not afraid of Veil. He did not need the vow. It was for me, my own peace of mind, and a bit of reckoning.

"Underground," I murmured. "I like it."

"Are you quite done playing games?" Veil sounded defeated, but I wondered if he truly was. Surely, he could break through the spell. He carried enough power for that.

"Are you healed?"

He flinched at my tone, and I wondered, too, what the ordeal at Hollow Forest had cost him. "I'm touched you're concerned for my well-being, Lord Freya. Now, would you kindly remove this vile curse from its hold?"

I did not smile at his use of the appeal. It was too serious a situation for fey games. "Release him."

Chevelle tossed sulfurous powder at Veil's feet and spoke

two clipped words. The vines melted into something tarry, pooling slowly over the stone.

"Get out," I said.

Veil gave me one long look before turning to go. I was grateful he'd not taken the time to leave a parting look with Chevelle. The fey lord strolled through the doorway into the corridor, and I heard the shifting and swords of two startled guards. I released an irritated breath.

Chevelle waited beside me, too still. He was angry, and Veil had likely done some damage beyond a scratch to his skin. The fey lord was blisteringly powerful, even off his own land, injured, and away from the base energy. My fingers trembled. I wanted nothing more than to sit down on the stone floor and cry. Instead, I curled my hands into fists and said, "Bring me Anvil."

6

JUNNIE

JUNNIE STARED DOWN AT THE MISSIVE BEFORE EXAMINING THE small scrap of flesh inside the glass vial. It was gray and brittle, something that seemed not quite fey. Aster and Ivy waited beside her in a narrow chamber deep within the largest of the new Council buildings. Its walls were cool and smooth, bare of the warmth and growth each of them so desperately needed. But it was not a task to leave to the forward rooms, where there was light and windows. The vial contained a secret that could get them all killed.

"Bury it," Junnie said. "We will ride out at dawn to inspect the full corpse."

Ivy stared up at her.

"Speak your piece," Junnie snapped.

Aster replied instead. "Surely, it would be best to go nowhere near the thing."

Junnie glanced between the two. It was clear that neither wanted anything to do with even the vial. "I don't want it coming for us. I want whatever this plague is nowhere near this village—any of our villages." She bit the inside of her lip, gesturing toward Aster. "Pack supplies to give us protection for the trip. I've no idea what Ruby will have left on hand." Junnie frowned.

She'd helped restore Ruby's stock after the fey attack, but the changeling Liana'd had access to everything in Ruby's rooms since then. Junnie motioned for her sentries to hurry but noticed Ivy's narrow brow still drawn down. The girl's long hair was knotted into a mass of braids at the nape of her neck, two shades brighter than the gilt threads of ivy trailing down her robe. Junnie had entrusted her with the task because she knew Ivy was cautious, but she needed her to see it through. "If you cannot do this, tell me now."

Ivy's mouth went into a flat line. "It is my honor to serve." She glanced at the vial then back at Junnie. "It is only that this seems unwise." *Unsafe.*

Junnie nodded. "It is. Very much so."

The girl sighed and, apparently appeased that the head of Council agreed with her assessment, leaned forward to carefully retrieve the vial from Junnie. She would bury it and complete their task.

"I'll have the horses readied," Junnie said. "Meet me in the stables as soon as it's done."

7

STEED

A BOOT KICKED SOLIDLY INTO THE SIDE OF STEED'S COT, AND HE crossed his arms to roll toward the stable wall. "Leave off, you brute. I've at least another hour of rest before duty calls."

Anvil snorted, leaning over to peer down at the side of Steed's face, at his single, slitted eye. "Not anymore," Anvil reported.

Steed opened the eye fully to glance at the other man.

"Aye," Anvil said. "You've gone and run your trap, and now we've a mission. Some wild quest to far-off lands." Steed raised a brow, but Anvil only glowered back down, as if maybe he was deciding whether to overturn the cot. "Why do you sleep in the stables when you've a suite fit for a lord inside?" He smirked, tilting his head as if leering under the edge of the cot. "Or 'ave you a lass under there—"

Steed's glare cut off the other man's words, but only because they were broken into a chuckle. "Where are we going?" he muttered.

Anvil crossed his arms. "You're not going to like it, but it's your own fault."

"Why do you keep saying that?" Steed ran a hand over his face, wondering exactly how many hours before dawn it truly was.

Anvil kicked a bag toward the cot, its contents clinking steel against steel. "So you remember whose fault it is when we're in the thick of it, that's why. Gather a team. I want Barris and whomever he deems fit. You can choose the rest."

Steed sat up, kicking his boot heels to the stone. He'd let muck dry on them despite his resolve to keep himself appropriately attired for one of his station. "How many? What's the task?"

"Aye," Anvil muttered. "I suppose you'll want breakfast before you hear that. And maybe a strong drink."

Steed frowned.

Anvil shook his head. "We're going to the wild. In search of beasties." As he turned to walk from the room, he called over his shoulder, "Better bring your sword."

$\sim$

"You're kidding," Steed said flatly, not for the first time since he'd sat at the table to breakfast with his longtime friend.

Anvil stared back at him, his expression making clear that he was not jesting in the least. "And how does she propose we pull this feat off? By what means?"

"Aye," Anvil agreed. "I suppose that's up to us now."

Steed blinked.

Anvil tore a hunk of bread into two.

They stared at each other.

"Merek," Steed said. "He's one of our best riders."

"Fast," Anvil agreed, "but not as quick as what he'll be chasing."

Steed frowned. "And what is it that Barris has, then? He's no faster than the rest of us."

"He knows the men." Anvil gestured with his bread, which dripped with whatever brown liquid he'd dipped it in. Steed hadn't bothered to look. Food was the last thing on his mind.

"I know the men," Steed said, "and none of them are equipped for this."

"Adventure, then." Anvil shrugged. "We sell them on the adventure. A name for themselves."

Steed scoffed. "Seems a poor legend to walk into your own death willingly."

"Honor," Anvil corrected with a slant to his brow. "I thought you were good at this sort of thing."

"This is no trade," Steed complained. "It's a give, and you know it. We'll be lucky to come back with half—" Steed cut himself off as Duer and Edan walked by. He gave them a small nod, then returned his gaze to his plate, untouched and unappealing. He pushed it away.

"We've no choice," Anvil said. "You know as well as the rest of us. If we don't find a cure for this"—he glanced around the room then returned his eyes to Steed—"whatever happens will be better than sitting in wait. Nothing good will come of the fey losing their source."

Steed knew it was true. The fey would spill onto elven territory, light and dark and then farther out, destroying everything in their path until the hunger for their absent energy was sated. It would be a slow, torturous death for as far as he had ever ridden on the land and for its inhabitants. "Barris," he said. "And Merek. We keep it small. I'll take on the risk myself if need be."

Anvil made a sound like a grunt, sliding Steed's plate into the place of his emptied one. "Barris and whoever Barris deems fit. I've no energy to go off leaping toward the sky. I like it here on the ground these days."

Steed closed his eyes for a long moment, hating the images that flashed through his mind. "Aye, Merek, Barris, and whoever he deems fit." The images went bad, so he opened his eyes again, training them on the other man. "We give them the choice. No one will walk into this without the option to have stayed."

Anvil smirked. "There's the infamous tradesman I've heard so much about." He gave a curt nod. "Agreed. They come on of their own will."

8

FREY

I WAS IN THE STUDY WHEN THE BODY SHOWED UP. I CROSSED MY arms over my chest, running a thumb over the cold ridge of the scar left by the teeth of the changeling's spellcast beasts on my forearm. "Seal the room," I commanded. I had already summoned Rhys and Rider, and Chevelle stood at my side.

Isa's sentries waited, straight and still, but I could see in their eyes that they were ready to be on their way.

"How many know of this?" I asked.

The tall, slender one—Taryn, I thought—stepped forward. "The package was disguised sufficiently."

I let my gaze stay on her. She was well aware the fey would be able to sniff it out.

She did not waver. "The details are in the missive."

"You know full well I've read it," I said flatly. "I want to know if the fey know we have this body."

"The missive—"

I tossed the scroll Isa had sent with her parcel onto the floor, the metal ring binding it clattering against the stone. "If

37

you've no intention of helping us resolve this, then be on your way."

Taryn turned automatically, the sentries at her sides spinning to follow. When I called to her, her steps paused, but she only glanced over her shoulder.

"Send our regards to Isa," I said. "Please let her know that while we may have been lax of late in properly monitoring and supporting her in her task, we will be certain to rectify that shortly."

Taryn's mouth tightened as she gave a short, single nod. When the door closed behind them, I pressed my fingers to the bridge of my nose.

"The fey barriers will hold," Chevelle said beside me.

I didn't bother reminding him that they had not held for the fey lord. "It doesn't matter if they followed her sentries. It matters that she's keeping it from us."

For Chevelle's part, he did not remind me that the only alternative to Isa was to hold the humans at bay myself. He knew I wouldn't be able to put a bargain sealed with a fey lord out of my mind for long. "This is beyond that concern," Chevelle said. "None of that will matter if the two are tied."

If this body was linked to the deadening of the land, he meant.

I blew out a breath, letting the energy making my palms itch crawl over my skin. I flicked my wrist, shaking out my hand before sliding it around the hilt of my sword. I missed the cold energy of my staff. Somehow, in less than a moon's time, I'd become attached to the feel of it, the security of a place to constantly tie my power. The staff was another thing I'd lost to the fey. The stone that held its focus had burst during my battle with the changeling, Pitt. But I could not say I regretted that fight, because we'd come close to losing more than just a stone. We'd nearly lost one of our Seven.

"Has someone checked on Ruby?"

Chevelle shifted closer to me. "You know we have."

"And Liana?"

"She's been sneaking off only briefly. It appears she still thinks we've no idea."

I nodded. "We will make them pay for this. You understand that."

Chevelle didn't answer, but I could feel his support beside me. He would follow me into the pits of Hollow Forest to see this done. He would stay by my side, even if it cost us everything we held dear.

I hoped it would not.

~

RHYS AND RIDER were silent as they entered, but I felt Chevelle shift to acknowledge them. I drew another deep drink of air, irritated that I had to remind myself to breathe. They came to rest beside us, concern apparent in their gazes. The brothers had been still, so purposeful in their movements when I'd first met them. They'd been with us long enough that their manner had softened a bit, their formality eased maybe not to the level of Steed, but at least to that of the head of our guard.

But the stillness had returned. Their shoulders were straight, their feet in a level line. They wore the black of the North, but their hair was as silver as ever. Rhys and Rider had been born of the ice lands, and when under stress, their responses—evidence to what they had been put through— swam to the surface.

"What I ask of you will not be without considerable risk." I let them see the truth in my gaze. Honesty was the only assurance I could give them. I would not hide the danger in what we were all about to undertake.

"We are here but to serve you, Lord Freya," Rhys said.

Rider inclined his head in agreement, both apparently beyond doubt in their duty.

I gestured Chevelle toward the table, where Isa's gift, draped with a gilded cloth and a dozen layers of twine and herbage, waited. I did not truly want him to touch it, but I could not ask it of one of my Seven and not the others.

As Chevelle drew the cloth free, it slid liquidly into a pile on the floor. Beneath it, suddenly bare, was the handiwork of Isa's sentries, light elves who swore by the protections of soil and flora. Rider's gaze slipped to mine then back to the table. On the base of the platform was a thin ridge of earth, but the wrappings over it did nothing to disguise the unmistakable shape of a body.

The brothers might have been from the ice lands, but they'd been studying fey since our first attack. They understood the method by which a fey body went, the way their energy returned to the earth, leaving nothing but husk or shell. What was before us was clearly not that.

"We've no idea if there is potential for the deadening to be spread from this," Chevelle said. The fey energy had been sapped from the being, and no one truly understood why.

Rhys took a step forward. "If this is where the deadening is headed, it will not matter. It will not be stopped by the spelled boundary."

Chevelle nodded then took a step away from the table as he crossed his wrists behind his back.

"May we?" Rider asked of the covering.

Chevelle gave me a glance, obviously wanting me away from the potential hazard despite his earlier words.

"Yes," I said.

Rider drew a blade from his belt, his capable hands guiding the tip of it over the form to slice only through the net of twine and top layer of pasted leaves and herbs. The scent of rosemary and lavender swelled through the room, followed by something more earthy and dark. Rhys pulled a pair of leather gloves from his belt then drew them over his slender hands. He gave a long look to his brother, and Rider slid the blade deeper through the layers. The smell of catmint and wormwood swam past, then marjoram and something so spicy it stung my nose. Soon, there was the rancid stench of decay, but only that of leaves and moss, not flesh. Not the body.

I blinked away the dampness welling at my eyes from the fumes, but Chevelle reached into a pouch at his waist then tossed dark ash toward the discarded leaves. It helped, but I did not step nearer. Rhys pulled back the last layer of flora, and the thin, gray corpse came into view.

She was fey, undoubtedly, and not one of the changelings who had been crossing over to play games on the land the humans occupied. She was a forest nymph, her hair still tipped with green, her clawed fingers meshed together with translucent webbing where they lay crossed over her sternum. Isa's sentries had left the broken twigs in her matted hair and the dried leaves plastered to her shoulder.

I leaned forward to study her face as Rhys and Rider moved slowly down the table. Her lips were pale and cracked, her lashes dark against her cheek. There were light scratches near her jaw, but the skin of her neck was clean. Her chest was sunken, her thin collarbones jutting out beneath the silks of her robes.

Someone had apparently stolen her gems. She did not appear to be wearing a single stone. I glanced at Chevelle, whose jaw was tight. "How long had she been lying there before Isa's men found her?" I asked.

His eyes met mine. "It can't have been long, if she's still in this condition."

"Then someone stole from her as the life drained from her body."

Rider stopped in his task to glance at me.

My look held him there. "When you're done with your study, see that she is returned to Veil." I turned from them, unable to stomach one more moment. The cold metal of the door handle met my palm, and I thought again how foolish I was.

The fey were not like us. They did not play by our rules. They would do things that might have made even someone like my grandfather turn away. The fey were not the sort of enemy we needed.

Even worse, we'd found them as our allies against the deadening of the energy, and there was nothing to be done for it.

It had been sealed as a bargain between two lords.

The nymph was not the last fey body I would find in my hands.

9

THEA

THEA WAS STARTLED FROM SLEEP, THE KNOCK OF WOOD AGAINST stone jarring her to sitting. She shoved the hair from her face, wide-eyed and blinking. Barris stared down at her, his mouth in an even line.

"What've you gotten into this time?" She groaned. "Please don't tell me it's something bad."

Barris crossed his arms. "It is never good, not when you're involved."

She snorted a laugh.

"Up," he said. "Edan wants to see you on the rampart by dawn."

She stared at him.

He nodded. "Aye. Better bring your sword." He wore a new chest plate and cloak, and what appeared to be thin black chainmail ran over his shoulders.

"Are you—" She paused, uncertain what he could be doing. Not going to battle, surely. They'd made peace with the light elves, and no other army would have made it that far without word reaching the castle guard.

"I've a mission," Barris answered. "It's confidential."

He said the last bit with a wink, but something was off in his tone. Something that Thea did not like lurked beneath the surface. She opened her mouth to tell him so, but movement at the doorway caught her eye.

She gaped.

Barris turned.

"Change of plans," the figure at the door said, and any hope Thea had of being wrong about who was in their presence was shattered by the unmistakable sound of the elven lord's voice.

Barris saluted, knocking his fist against his chest and dipping his head.

"Clear the barracks," Freya told him.

Barris filed out behind the remaining few, who had hastily grabbed their things without a single word.

Thea swallowed. She was certain she should stand and salute, but a cold ball of dread had settled in her stomach. The Lord of the North and the Dark Elves' Kingdom had just emptied her barracks to see Thea alone.

Something was wrong. Something bad.

The Lord of the North—Freya, Thea reminded herself— took a step forward. She seemed pale in the flickering torch-light, and Thea felt as if something dangerous swam beneath those strange green eyes.

"I need to know if I can trust the changeling," Freya said. At Thea's raised brow, she added, "Trust her to let Ruby heal without your daily supervision. Trust her to play no more games with our guard."

No one could truly trust a changeling, not completely. The changeling Liana had saved Steed and the others after their clashes with the fey. Those had been pawns to her, whom she'd needed to play out her game.

Thea could not say that the woman needed Ruby, and

apparently, neither could Freya, or she would not be asking. "I've seen nothing amiss," Thea admitted. After a moment of contemplation, she said, "But I did not like the methods she used on Steed." Her gaze shot to her lord. "They did work. I only—"

She didn't have to finish. Freya nodded. She'd seen it too.

Thea bit her lip. "I could give Ruby something to wake her. But if it were too soon…" She shook her head. "I can't imagine why the changeling would risk it beneath your nose. And Grey's there. He's been witness to her concoctions long enough to suspect when something is wrong."

Frey gave another curt nod. "Done, then. Leave instructions for the tonic with Grey, should he find he needs to use it."

Thea took a slow breath. "Have I—have I done something wrong?"

Frey's chin tilted for a moment, then she shook her head. She glanced at the empty barracks before her gaze came back to Thea's. "No, you've done well. I need you for something else."

Thea nodded automatically, but the tightness in the pit of her stomach grew. Barris's tone had been off. Frey's tone was off, as was the way she looked at Thea. There was a darkness in Frey's eyes. Thea swallowed hard. "What happened?"

Frey's mouth fell into a tight line. She seemed to draw a steadying breath. "I'm going to ask too much of you, but I'm afraid there's nothing for it."

Thea shifted the blanket off her lap and stood to face her lord.

"I need a healer," Frey said. And then the Lord of the North stepped forward to take hold of Thea's hands. "I need you to bring them back alive."

THEA

THEA MET STEED AND THE OTHERS OUTSIDE THE STABLES AS they prepared to mount and be on their way. They had packed light, as if it would be a short journey, and Thea felt suddenly chagrined about the large sack she carried over her shoulder. Steed dropped the leather strap he'd been adjusting on his saddle, shooting Barris a look that Thea could not exactly decipher. Barris gave a furtive shake of his head, and Steed turned to face Thea.

She came to a stop in front of him.

He glanced at her pack, his dark gaze coming back to hers. "No."

"She said you'd say that." Thea thrust a folded slip of paper toward him. Thea had not opened the note, but she knew it was brief. The Lord of the North had only scribbled a few short words before handing it over.

Steed read it twice and pinched the bridge of his nose. After a moment, his fingers curled over the note, folding it tighter before he stuffed it into a pocket. He took a slow breath as he stared at her. He reached up to pluck the metal clasp that marked her as a member of the castle guard off her shoulder then tossed it toward a crate of supplies near the stable door. "This goes," he ordered, gesturing toward the metal bracer at her wrist. "And this." He jerked the metal buckle of her shoulder strap loose. His eyes skirted her face as he took in her hair, the tip of the bow peeking over her back. "Leave it," he said of the bow.

She tossed her pack on the ground, settling the weapon beside it. Steed turned to one of the stable hands, gesturing with some signal Thea did not understand as he moved toward the stable doors. When he disappeared, the new recruit who'd been helping Ruby approached.

Willa was petite, nearly Ruby's size, and lean but strong. Her arms were bare between a dark leather vest and long leather bracers. Her glossy black hair was cropped and spiky, and her dark eyes tipped up at the edges. Her mouth was set in a hard line. "Put that thing down if you're not going to learn how to use it."

Thea gripped the handle of her sword, taken aback by the girl's words. Her tone had not been harsh, but it still felt like a command.

"You will only get tangled in it," the girl snapped. "It will do you no good. The daggers are all you need."

Thea towered over the girl, and yet, Thea felt somehow small. She glanced at Barris, who stood watching with a sick sort of look in his eyes, as if haunted by that *something bad* they'd all been hiding. Thea hadn't understood before, but her doubt was gone. She knew the risk they were taking. She unlatched the scabbard from her side and placed the sword with her other weapons. She felt a bit bare with nothing but daggers, but she reminded herself that she wasn't going along to fight. She was going along to stitch warriors back together.

Willa bent down to grab Thea's pack, tossing it over her

shoulder as Steed came from the stables with a large black mare. Willa met him to attach the pack, her posture that of a soldier, as it had been every single time Thea had seen her. Steed adjusted the saddle and checked the pack before glancing briefly at Thea. Her stomach dipped, more ill at ease than she'd ever been, but she forced her trembling hands to steady and took a deep breath. It would not be the worst she'd done, surely. She climbed onto the mare and pressed her heels against the beast's sides, following Steed, Barris, Merek, and Willa in their columns.

It was still early, and as they rode through the castle grounds, no one paid them any mind. At the gate, Anvil waited with his own horse, exchanging a look with Steed before falling in line beside Thea. Anvil was a massive man, broad and tall and not easy to forget. Thea wondered at their removal of their guard identifiers, as if any of the Seven could possibly go unnoticed, in uniform or out. But then she looked closer at what they did wear and thought maybe she'd been mistaken about why they'd removed the gear. Even Barris, who'd been wearing mail only earlier that morning, was stripped down to dark leather and a woven shirt. When they'd faced the fey, they'd been covered in metal, wanting to ward off the magic that was within their foes, but they'd stripped all of it clean.

Because they would not be fighting against magic—they would be fighting to stay alive.

~

IT WAS three days of hard riding before they saw the first sign of a dragon: the charred bones of large prey. Two days later, dark shadows swept the clouds. By the evening of the sixth day, Thea was more exhausted than she'd ever been, sore, missing a proper bath and bed, and a bit ill-tempered. The way had been clear enough for the most part, as Steed had guided them through well-used paths over level ground. They'd only stopped a few times to change horses, making quick trades that Steed must have sent word for ahead of their departure.

Unlike the wooded lands of the South or the thick fey forests, the grasslands they rode through were populated by wild game and the occasional band of rogues. Farther out, there would be imp settlements and the rocky lands of the orcs and ogres. Thea had never seen those lands herself, but she'd heard enough tales to know which were true. She had no interest in going that far.

She climbed down from her horse, too tired to notice where she'd stopped until her boots hit the sloppy give of mud. She groaned, staring down to find it splattered well up her pant leg. Barris chuckled, taking her horse and leading it with the others to a smattering of trees past where Merek and Anvil had started making camp. The sun was low in the sky, but it seemed to take longer to dip below the horizon. She could see far into the distance, even in the strange rosy light. Thea glanced over her shoulder at the others. They'd taken to a bit of a routine with their tasks. Each night, Anvil and Merek set up camp while Barris brought water to the horses and Willa scouted the area for tracks or bones. Steed would hunt and upon his return check the horses while Merek cooked whatever game he'd been able to find. Thea, it seemed, wasn't meant for any of their official duties. She frowned at the lot of them, not for the first time, and wandered toward the lake, where some brush looked promising for berries that were either edible or medicinal.

She'd been warned not to wander off, not to cause any havoc to their carefully laid plans. She snorted, shifting the leaves to verify the sort of plant on which the berries grew. They were shadeberries, not edible. She plucked one off the bush to split it with her thumbnail, careful of thorns, but the fruit wasn't even ripe enough to add to a soap. She missed a good-smelling soap.

Thea glanced at her pant legs, splattered with mud that was quickly drying in the warm air, and noted exactly how much was clumped on her boots. She shook her head, kicking a heel to loosen it before deciding to move farther into the grasses, toward the edge of the lake. The stone there was light and sandy, and she used it to scrape the larger chunks free before she dipped her heels in and wiped them clean. Chore accomplished, Thea knelt by the edge of the water to wash the berry pulp and mud from her hands. She heard the distant sound of Merek's laughter and smiled. Merek had joined the guard when Thea had, so not only had she grown up with him in Camber, but she'd trained with him for a season. His family was of the best sort, kind and giving and always ready with a laugh. Barris seemed reserved in comparison, but they got along well.

Thea dug a bit of dirt from beneath her fingernail then leaned forward to wash the remnants clean. The setting sun threw color across the water's still surface, but beneath it something dark slid from the depths, smooth and—

Thea screeched as she was jerked backward, falling onto her rear as Steed let go of her vest. He stepped in front of her, blade in hand as the dark mass rose slowly to the surface, cresting its slick black head to peer at them with one golden eye. Steed waited, motionless, and the thing blinked before rolling onto its side and sliding back into the depths, smooth skin and sharp claws quietly breaking the surface as it spun.

Thea panted, watching in horror, and after a moment, Steed turned to stare down at her. "Thea."

She shook her head. "I know, I know. My only duty is to stay *out* of trouble."

He slid his blade into its scabbard. "This isn't home. Nothing here is governed by law. Beast and man alike live by the rule of the wild."

"Eat or be eaten?" she muttered.

He held a hand out, and she took it, allowing him to pull her to her feet. She'd been shaken and was exhausted, but it was really the first chance she'd had to be so close to Steed and practically alone. A small thrill ran through her at his nearness, but she resisted the urge to reach for him. Steed was on a mission, a mission he'd clearly not wanted her to be a part of.

She understood why. She cleared her throat. "So dinner, I guess."

Steed's gaze strayed from hers, trailing slowly to her mouth. He seemed drawn to her, and she felt the same subtle shift coming from him that had her leaning his way, but there was a sound from the camp, and his eyes flicked to the distance behind her. He reached forward, tugging gently on the hem of her shirt as he whispered, "Please stay close. And do try not to get eaten."

Thea bit back a grin as he strode past her toward the camp. And then her gaze caught on the murky water, and she hurriedly turned to follow him in.

～

"THEY'RE CLOSE," Willa said as Steed approached the camp. Thea kept pace behind him, trying to decipher what sort of meat Anvil had spitted over the fire.

"Three or more," the girl told Steed, "signs no more than a day old."

Steed nodded. "We go at first light, in hopes they're still asleep."

Anvil made the sign of the elders, who used to make a quick, circular gesture to ward off talk of curses.

Thea smiled. She hadn't thought of the elders in a long while. So many of them had been lost in the massacre, targeted, taken down. Her smile faded, and she shook off the thought as she made her way to the fire.

Willa intercepted her, gesturing toward Thea's blades. "Let's have a go with those," she said.

Thea frowned.

The girl stared up at her, unflinching. "It's time to learn. You've not trained once since leaving the castle."

Merek snickered, but Barris managed to tamp down his grin.

"Come," Willa said, gesturing again. "I'll show you how to throw."

Thea didn't think she'd heard the girl speak so much in the entire time she'd been exposed to her.

Willa pointed toward the thin trees beside the camp. "That one's dead. Hit it center"—she raised her hand—"this high, and I'll trust you can use them well enough."

Thea crossed her arms. "Did someone bet or dare you into this much talking?"

Willa glared up at her. The look said plenty, and Thea thought maybe she preferred the girl when actually speaking. "Fine," Thea said. She drew a knife, holding it loosely in one hand as she readied her grip.

"Not that one," Willa said. "It's meant for close-quarters stabbing." She pointed to the thin dagger at Thea's thigh. "Use the proper blade."

Merek glanced at Barris, while Anvil only stood with his arms crossed before the fire, apparently paying the discussion no mind. Steed was farther out, running a hand over the legs of the horses to check for any potential issues caused by the extended ride.

Thea took hold of the proper blade, glancing at Willa for further comment, only to find none. She focused on the tree ahead, hating how near to its path Anvil stood, and steadied her grip. She tossed, relieved that it stuck nearly in the right spot.

Willa shook her head.

"What?" Thea snapped. "It's right there."

Willa turned to face her, making a small circle with her hands. "A deadly strike has to be this accurate, at least. You've killed nothing but yourself, because at this range you've no time to reset."

Thea blinked.

"Again," Willa said. She held her hand out, drawing the knife to her with startling precision. Willa snapped it out of the air and passed it handle-first to Thea.

Thea cleared her throat and took a steadying breath. Willa turned to mirror her posture, sliding her feet slightly wider and her shoulder to the side. Thea followed the girl's example, taking aim again as Willa adjusted her grip.

The sixth time, she hit near enough that Willa seemed satisfied. The girl nodded curtly, facing Thea. "Hit that spot a dozen times a night, and you'll eventually be decent at something, at least."

Thea's mouth dropped open.

Merek laughed full-out at her expression, though Willa's face showed no signs of humor. Merek elbowed Barris at his side and shook his head. "Curses," he said through laughter, "I'm so glad you chose her for this mad jaunt."

Barris went still. Thea's gaze flicked from one man to the other. Merek, apparently realizing his mistake, straightened sheepishly as he shared a glance with Barris. Thea remembered a similar exchange between Barris and Steed.

Thea stared at her friend. "You… You were the one who decided who would go?"

Barris wet his lips.

"Only her," Merek said. "Anvil chose Barris here, and Steed chose me."

Barris gave Merek a look that clearly said he wished the man would shut his trap.

"So you chose Willa," Thea said, "over me."

Barris went pale. To his credit, he did not attempt a lie.

"I wouldn't have let him take you in any case," Steed said from behind them. He'd left the horses and was moving toward the group. Steed had informed her he'd not wanted her along before they'd even left the castle, but Thea thought she felt more betrayed by Barris than anyone. She shoved the dagger into its sheath, unable to meet his steady gaze. He wasn't wrong, though—she could barely use a weapon. She had a single skill, and it was the only reason she'd been allowed to go along. She shifted, wanting to say *something*.

A wind blew through the clearing, the leaves shivering on their thin branches, and the lot of them went still. Anvil watched the sky, and Thea realized just how dark it had become. Her hand tightened where it still rested around the hilt of her dagger.

"They're a day or so out?" Merek whispered.

Willa only shrugged. She'd been looking at the ground, after all. There was no telling how far and how fast the creatures could fly.

Thea really, really wished she'd taken more time to study up on dragons before she'd agreed to come along. Steed carefully unfastened his sword belt, and Merek was moving toward his pack. Thea realized she'd no idea how they planned to catch the thing, but apparently it involved a length of spelled rope and leaving their weapons on the ground.

"Wait," Thea hissed. "Why not just drug it?"

Steed's eyes did not leave the sky. "Do you know how much tonic it takes to sedate a dragon?"

She pressed her lips together.

"Maybe you should shift carefully under the shelter of those trees," he said.

She might have argued with him—about the trees being enough to shelter her or the fact that he'd asked her to step clear of the fight, she wasn't sure—but there was a strange shush of air that she could only imagine was a second dragon overhead. Her feet moved automatically, for once not dumping her directly into the fight.

She thought it was absolutely mad. Thea watched the others, clear of any weapons or belts that might snag on their prey. They would be wrangling a wild beast larger than all of them combined. Steed was right. She'd no idea what it would take to drug a beast that size into stupor—but even if she did, she supposed they'd have to find a way to haul it back. They'd been riding for six days, and it would take at least twice that to get back. Maybe more.

Madness. And they'd only just begun.

FREY

JUNNIE'S COMPANIONS, BOTH WOMEN TALL AND GOLDEN, THEIR hair in crowns of braid, lowered their hoods. I let my eyes meet Junnie's and was not at all reassured by what I saw there.

"Clear the hall." My words echoed against the stone walls, and Kieren did as I bid. Chevelle moved to stand beside me, his presence the only thing steadying about the entire ordeal.

In the quiet stillness, Junnie said, "Isa sent a missive."

"We received something a bit more substantial." My tone was dry, but Junnie's expression made clear she knew exactly what had been delivered.

"We would like to examine it ourselves, if such is possible."

I gave a curt nod. "Rhys and Rider have only just finished. My intent is to return it to its owner by the summer festival."

Junnie blinked. "That does seem fitting, I suppose." She was silent a moment, likely imagining the fey lord's reaction to such a public gift. "Yes," she said. "And after we've done our own survey, perhaps Ivy and Aster can discuss their findings with Rhys and Rider."

I felt Chevelle's surprise beside me, but only in the tiny

flinch of his hand. The light elves were notorious for their disinterest in sharing knowledge of that sort. What was made available in their libraries had been carefully chosen and consistently overseen. Any knowledge of real value was hidden within the labyrinth of rooms deep inside the Council buildings.

I inclined my head, pleased with Junnie's offer, and she added, "I would also like a moment with you while they discourse."

Privately, she meant. "Of course," I answered. "Chevelle will show you to the room where the fey is being held. And afterward, my study."

Junnie dipped her head. It wasn't exactly a subordinate gesture, but certainly nothing like how she'd ever reacted to the previous Lord of the North.

∽

IT WAS late in the day when we finally met in my study. Junnie's cloak was draped over her shoulder, her hands freshly washed. She smelled of rosemary and eucalyptus, and I had the feeling the body of the fey had been as chilling to her as it had to the rest of us. Chevelle gave me a long look from the entrance before he closed the door, but I knew whatever was said would be private. He did not particularly like any member of Council, but Junnie had saved me more than once. And it was not the old Council. It was only her.

She sat carefully in the chair beside me, her pale hair out of place in the flickering light of the study. Everything about her seemed wrong there. Junnie belonged to the sun, to the light. She frowned. "The examination was sufficiently unpleasant."

I nodded. "Had I known you were coming, we would have

waited. Your men did well with their preservation, but I'm afraid it's been a bit too long."

Junnie sighed. "It was not our intention. We ran into a little trouble on the route." At my raised brow, she shook her head. "Nothing I haven't already dealt with."

"I'm sure it hasn't been easy."

The corner of her mouth tugged into a tight smile. "I don't suppose I ever thought it would be. But it was time for a change."

Indeed. The old Council had been murderous and manipulative. But that was not what Junnie had come to discuss. "I was surprised, to say the least, when your men delivered the fey body here."

Any hint of relaxation slid from Junnie's face. "Maybe not my men. It seems their allegiance has shifted in their time outside of our own lands."

I tapped a finger to the leather binding of a history of the ancients. I'd not shown Junnie the other book, the one Rhys and Rider had found, regarding the wolves and the boundary. I wasn't sure why. Finn and Keaton were no secret, and Junnie seemed more in touch with them than even I. And yet, she'd held her connection with them close to her chest, like so much else. It was time to move past that. We were fighting a bigger enemy than either of us could face alone.

I would let my questions come free. "And what of Isa?"

Junnie's expression was uncomfortable as she replied. "I have great love for her but I cannot say that I entirely trust her." Her long fingers ran over the threads of her cloak. "It is an unsettling sort of feeling."

I let out a mirthless huff of air. "And yet, I am the lord of your people's enemies." Not just me, but also my mother and hers before—Junnie's own sister had chosen to live in the North among the dark elves.

Junnie's eyes, bright and clear, met mine. "They are not our enemy. The discontent was driven by the actions of one man." Her mouth turned down at one corner. "And you know as well as I do that our kind had as much wrongdoing as he."

My hand stilled its fidgeting at Junnie's words. *Our kind.* Because regardless of how I felt about the land where I was born and the elves who surrounded me, I was her blood too. My mother and her forebears were light elves, even if my own mother was half Asher's bloodline and dark elf. Junnie considered me one of hers.

I leaned toward Junnie, the only one left of my kin outside of the girl, Isa, whom Junnie was trying to save. "Asher knew how the ancient boundaries interfered with fey powers. He'd been studying the energy of all kinds. He wanted me." But I wasn't enough. With the influence of my mother, I'd refused to fall into line. "He wanted me to use an army of humans. And for what?" I shook my head. "The changelings are not the only beings at fault. And we've no idea if the deadening is even due to the humans at all. What if Asher's meddling with the darkness set the whole thing afoot?"

Junnie's gaze was steady on mine. "You call it darkness."

"It is."

"And yet—"

Her words fell off at my expression, but I would not discuss it. The secret was not mine to share.

Junnie's expression softened. "There is no reason to hide it. Not any longer. The threats to you both are gone."

They'd been replaced by new threats, dangers that dealt with the very core of what Asher had done. I ignored her urging. "Asher studied the boundaries the ancients laid in place to discover how they affected fey magic. He studied the methods with which to transfer and bind." He'd wanted me to bring down his enemies, wanted me at his side. He'd gone as far as to hurt Chevelle to get to me and had tried to turn me against my own mother. I'd taken it personally. I'd missed his grander plan. "Whatever he discovered, the fey now know."

"I will pay the spellcaster recompense for what he has done." Junnie's words were cold. "Your concern will be how to resolve your bargain with the fey lord."

"Spellcasters," I corrected. Junnie's brow drew together, and I explained, "Veil paid us a visit several weeks ago. Apparently, there is more than one."

Her gaze darkened for just a moment. "What else?"

I crossed my arms. "He stole a gem from my own private collection."

"That cursed ruby again?"

"No." I started to explain my theory, but Junnie winced.

"What is that?" she asked.

My study was deep inside the castle, well insulated from sound, and yet, a strange screeching reached us, muffled by stone. I tended to forget the others had better hearing than I, but usually by the time someone noticed, my guard had sounded a call. This was something else.

I stood, feeling a strange sort of brush in my mind. Distress. Anger. "Junnie," I breathed, "I think you've come to us just in time."

VEIL

THE FEY HAD NEVER POSTPONED A FESTIVAL, NOT EVEN WHEN their entire world was in peril, and that was how Veil found himself preparing to be encircled by a mass of dancing, costumed revelers as they celebrated the change of season. Summer was coming, whether he was ready for it or not.

His new home was finished, grander and more opulent than the last, but he stood instead in a narrow chamber of the lair, fastening jewels to the cuffs on his arm. Liana found him there, shirtless and brooding, when she entered a place in which she'd no business being.

Veil glanced at her and could not help but shake his head. She'd shown up in a gown of elven royalty, complete with black-leather bracers and braided hair. "This is what you chose for the first festival of summer?"

She swirled the inky skirt around her, and Veil could swear he heard a smile in her voice. "Do you like it? I thought it would make a wonderful display."

He slid an emerald ring onto his first finger, carved citrine on his second. "It will certainly attract attention."

Liana stepped closer, examining his healing wound and then the pile of stones on the table. She leaned forward, and he could smell the herbs on her. She must have come straight from caring for the halfling, no doubt flying with her pixies. Her eyes caught on the dragonstone.

Veil slipped it into his palm then turned to face her, sliding the gem to a pocket. "What brings you into my private quarters this day, changeling?"

She frowned at him, and he nearly felt regret at the reminder of what she was until she said, "I thought you preferred visits this way."

He did not know if she was referring to his recent call in the elven lord's private chambers or the fact that he'd meant to keep his associations with Liana private, but he didn't like either implication. "I have a festival to bring underway," he told her. His eyes strayed to the collar of her gown, buttoned up the length of her neck. She had that color again, that blush of ripe summer fruit that was not truly hers.

She smiled at him, her eyes dark. "That's why I'm here, of course. I would not miss the summer festival." Her own gaze trailed over him, across bare collarbone and shoulder to the jewels on his arm. "It's always been my favorite."

He would not be drawn into her games. He picked up his shirt from where it had been draped over a chair and slipped the thin garment over his arms, but Liana only moved closer, her fingers deftly fastening the buttons adorned with gems.

"Maybe you're right," she said. "Maybe this dress is all wrong for the festival. What do you think, something in red?"

He turned to tell her he did not care, to make clear her place, but her hair had gone from amber braids to short golden waves. She was so powerful, he could feel it. Keane and Pitt had not been stronger than Liana—it was only that she'd not been able to fight them both on her own. The elves did not understand that. They thought her weak. She was nothing of the sort.

Liana had never been lacking in power, but on fey land, near the source, she felt as if she was more dangerous than any of his foes. And yet they'd trusted her within their castle walls, just as she stood within his own.

"Tell me how you draw on the base magic outside fey lands." His voice was nearly a whisper, though he'd meant nothing of the sort. She was near him again, closer than she'd any right to be. "What is it?" he asked. "A spring? A crack? A stone?" He would not say the other. He would not ask if it had been spellcast.

She grinned, her teeth flat and straight and very unlike fangs. "Ask me something else."

Her cheeks flushed pink, and despite his resolve, he murmured, "Let me see you."

The color fell with her grin, but she did not move away. He'd no right to ask it, even as the lord of the fey, but he wanted to see her true form. He wanted to see her bare.

"And if I do?"

He gave a small shake of his head, not taking his gaze from hers. "No bargains. Freely or not at all."

She bit the edge of her lip as if being coy, as if the idea that she would ever give something freely was daring. He knew her better than that, even if it felt like he knew her not at all.

There was a sound in the passageway, and Veil gave her one last look, one last chance. When she only stared back at him, he said, "I have to get to the festival."

"I will see you there." She gestured toward the length of gown that nearly trailed along the floor. "I have to change first."

Veil purposefully glanced at the shelf of gems before turning to stride from the room.

~

CYREN AND KEL waited at the end of the passageway, each suited in finery the color of primrose and red yarrow. They'd twined thin crowns into their hair, fashioned after the fey lord's own, and lined their eyes with kohl. Veil strode past them as together they turned, following him out past the dozen high-fey guards, each of whom had let Liana pass.

He would deal with that later. He kicked off the earth without care for grace, bursting through the canopy to fly above the trees. The sky was lightening already, sunrise so close that he could feel it beneath his skin. The ceremony would wait for him, but the fey court was anything but patient. He flew straight and true, and when he finally landed among the revelers, it was to their riotous cheers. There, he felt grounded. There, he understood exactly who he was.

FREY

WE MOVED SWIFTLY DOWN THE CORRIDOR, OUR FEET SILENT ON age-old stone. Junnie's dog had been waiting silently outside my study door, immediately trailing after Junnie and me, the massive beast's ears pointed at some sound my own could not hear. Echoed shouts from the outer wall reached us as we cleared the interior walls, and in the courtyard, castle guards struggled to keep their gazes on task.

I supposed I should have warned them.

Junnie's stride was longer than mine, but she did not hurry past me. I wondered if she could tell what awaited us, as I could. But her eyes were pinched at the corners, as if struggling to reach what felt nearer to me every step. "Surely, you can feel it," I said.

She glanced at me, her gaze sharp. She could not, apparently.

My steps slowed. "Junnie, the wolves. You can speak to them."

She shook her head. "Of course not." A screech tore through the air, and Junnie glanced toward the battlements. "I can indeed sense their ideas, or maybe 'direction' is a more apt term. But I cannot speak to their minds." She scoffed. "Certainly would have saved a lot of trouble these past few seasons if I could."

I stared at her. It was as if she knew the beast was out there, but that was all. She couldn't reach it.

Her expression said she was tired of waiting, so I gave her a small smile as we continued. When we finally reached the outer walls, I was surprised to see how far away the lot of them were. My awe stilled as I tried to make out the figures, praying silently that each of them was there. I turned to hurry down to meet them and caught Junnie's gaping stare.

Her blue eyes slid from the group to mine. "Yes," I said to her astonishment. "That is exactly what I have done."

"The gem," Junnie said. "You said Veil stole a gem from you."

I nodded. "Dragonstone."

"And so…"

I shrugged. "I'm going to let Rhys and Rider study him. See if they can discern how the power works. How its energy flows and how it feeds from the source."

Junnie's gaze caught on something behind me, and I turned, finding Chevelle. He stood on the balustrade, staring out at the beast and his guard. His gaze came to me, as if he could feel me watching him, and I wondered if what I saw in his expression was awe—Not for a wild, captured beast, but for me.

I smiled at him. He smirked.

A brush of distress, hot and searing, cut through any feeling of triumph. "Let's go," I told Junnie. "They need our help."

WE MET my guard on the rocky slope that led to the least-used paths to the castle. The way was treacherous but less populated than the other routes. Junnie and I dismounted our horses to greet the group, my senses screaming as the beast struggled against spelled rope and six men. The creature was enormous, towering over even mounted soldiers. It was hard to take my eyes from the animal, but then I found Steed, bloodied and bruised, his shirt torn at the neck. Anvil rode opposite him, anchoring the dragon's massive head from the other side. It was not a small feat, as even the beast's head dwarfed Anvil in size.

Behind Anvil rode Merek, who seemed relatively clean, and Barris, who had a thoroughly bandaged arm. Farther back rode Thea and Willa, each holding ropes that attached behind the dragon's neck, stretched taut over its bound wings and weighted tail. Alive, all of them. The relief I felt at the sight brought an unpleasant realization that I'd not expected as much.

I stepped forward, and Junnie's dog whined quietly as her direction held him back. I glanced at her, just to gauge her reaction against my own. A soft laugh escaped me with a breath of air. When she looked at me, I said, "Junnie, I've never asked. What have you named this beast of a dog?"

Her brow shifted at my odd question, but she said, "I've not chosen one yet."

I nodded. "I've not named my hawk, either. I'm sure one will come."

The dragon screeched, its cry ripping through the hazy mountain air to reverberate over stone. My guard drew to a stop in a clearer spot of ground, carefully unwinding their ropes from saddles to take them in hand. Steed leapt free of his horse, only to immediately be yanked toward Anvil's side as the dragon bucked and twisted. The three on the far side moved backward as the three on Steed's side worked to regain control. Tiny little Willa dug in, shouting commands at Thea, who herself was being pulled by the beast. It rolled again, snaking its body so that a bound wing caught on the rope, the wing claws snapping one line free as the bulk of the beast's back leg slammed into Merek.

The creature was angry, I could feel it. It was frustrated, exhausted. It wanted to be free. I reached for Junnie, wishing again that I had my staff, and held on for support as I threw myself toward the mind of the dragon. I expected it to be the hardest thing I'd ever done, that it would hurt worse than the humans, that it would be impossible to even reach, let alone control. But it felt so close—so much like a familiar, easy thing.

I fell into its mind, melting seamlessly with what seemed not so different from my birds, though it was an entirely incomparable thing. But the ease with which I felt it, the simplicity of that connection, was one that I had known all of my years.

I sighed, opening my eyes to find the dragon entirely still, standing in place as it watched me. Its chest swelled and fell in rumbling breaths, scenting the air with sulfur. I stepped closer, staring up at its intelligent eyes as it huffed a breath at me through the long slits in its nose. The creature had leathery wings beneath its bindings and sharp spikes lining its neck and back. They trailed down the center of a scaled reptilian body, black with hints of a deep, dark red. Its tail was long and presumably barbed at the end, based on the way it had been wrapped in twine.

I startled as a loud clang sounded in the silence—Anvil drove a spike into the ground to tie off his rope. Steed did the same on the opposite side, and then the others followed, walking warily forward and past the dragon's head. It must have been the most dangerous part, for they'd bound its snout in several layers of the spelled material, only leaving it room to breathe.

"You're safe now," I carefully told my guard.

Thea stepped past Steed to stare at me for a moment before her eyes trailed to the dragon and back again. "You mean…" Her hands came up to her hips. She blinked, the smear of blood over her temple crusted into her brow. "You could have just done this from the start?"

Steed, for once, did not reprimand her for speaking out of turn.

"I did not know," I said truthfully. I could not have anticipated it. I had only thought to study the creature's power from the outside, not that it would be possible to reach inside its mind.

"Have you never been exposed to one?" Junnie asked.

I shook my head. "When I was a child. But from a distance. I never thought—"

"What is it like?" Junnie's voice was low, reverent.

"Like nothing I've ever felt," I whispered, "and yet, so much like my birds."

She hummed, and I wondered if she—like me—was thinking about how each of us had a stronger connection to our favored beasts and what that meant.

Barris made to cross his arms over his chest, only to drop them again when he brushed his bandaged wounds.

"I'm sorry," I said. "We've secured a place in the keep. I'll take the dragon there. Please come in for rest and tending." My gaze met Thea's. "I trust everyone is well?"

She frowned, which was not entirely out of character. "We've a few burns I'd like to have looked at." She let her words trail off, obviously questioning whether Ruby was awake without saying it outright.

I gave a small shake of my head.

Junnie stepped forward. "Come," she said. "I can look at them. We brought fresh supplies from our gardens and some new varieties I believe will be of much use to you, Thea."

Thea glanced at Steed briefly before moving to follow Junnie, but his eyes were on me, waiting for orders. He looked tired, and I felt some regret for it.

"Thank you," I told him.

Anvil chuckled, standing at the men's sides as Willa kept a watchful gaze on the dragon. "Aye," Anvil said. "His reward will be legend."

I smiled, finally letting the scope of what they'd accomplished sink in. "Like no other," I agreed.

That was to say nothing of what might happen once the fey found out.

1 4

VEIL

THE FESTIVAL THAT USHERED IN THE SUMMER SEASON WAS A bright and raucous thing. The sun was low in the sky, and the revelers were unrestrained, feral with drink and dust. Veil had allowed himself wine but managed to restrain himself from partaking in much of the revelry. The spellcasters would have been fools to show themselves among a crowd of high fey—those who knew the changelings' intent was not to save the entire kind from an ill fate, but only themselves. Not that the fey would hold the self-serving changelings to task, but they would be captured or killed for their valuable information, for the *how* of the exchange of power.

Two fey women danced before Veil's dais, their energy tingling against his own, warm and inviting. He had been presented with more than food and flesh—at the base of his dais rested piles of offerings for the pleasure of the lord of the court, including rare gems and roots, fine clothes and seeds, thick pelts, and crowns of carved antler. He would share the spoils with his guard and decorate his new palace with their splendor, but he did not truly care for those things.

A fire fey sent a flame to dance overhead and laughed when the wind blew it into sparks and ash. Three frost monsters clung together, stumbling into a fall as one when the first caught his robe on the spear of a drunken warrior. Two tall females danced, their wings intertwined, as another watched from below, her thin fingers playing along with the movement. Beyond them, a fight broke out, the crowd laughing and jeering as a wood nymph knocked a man to the ground. The fey surrounding the prone man surged forward, their energy swelling within Veil.

The fates' dance had replenished the energy that fed them all, and Veil felt almost drunk with the power that swam through him. Even with the darkness that threatened them, Veil's connection to the base energy was stronger there, made more potent by the willing release of so many fey. He let the power fill him then released it once more. His skin felt alive, his chest alight. He wanted to join the others, to dance, to drink, to do much, much darker things.

Across the court floor, shimmering sapphire caught his eye. It was not a usual hue for a summer festival and certainly not meant to blend in. The gown was long and layered, silken strips floating over the lean legs that moved beneath it. Her feet were bare on the warm, flat stones, her arms and neck exposed to the last rays of sun. Her hair was long and loose, more white than blond, her face a sharper angle, her lips soft and full. But her eyes were as black and depthless as ever.

She did not smile as she crossed the court, and it only made his blood run hotter. He could not stop the images of her running through his mind of slender fingers grazing the flesh of his thigh, claws pressing into his back, the way she would move beneath him, and the taste of ripe summer fruit on her skin.

His hand twitched to beckon her, to call her to the dais in

front of everyone. But he did not need the spectacle. He wanted her alone.

He could not say it was shame. What he felt was something more possessive. It had started the moment they had brushed energy, when they had pulled the halfling fey from the fires of Hollow Forest.

Liana stopped midway across the floor, drawing a cloak off an unaware reveler before pulling it tightly over her exposed shoulders. Her gaze held something far from his own, and Veil shifted uncomfortably in his seat. He tasted the bitter tang of barberries and regretted partaking in wine.

Cyren leaned forward slightly, eyes on a watersprite in the crowd. Kel, beside him, ran his fingertip over the rim of a tall glass of wine, his nail long and narrow and dripping red. Among the crowd, a bawdy song took root, spreading like fire through the drunken revelers. A voice nearer Veil picked up the tune, ringing out high and sweet and impossible to ignore.

He made the effort.

Liana's gaze trailed from Veil toward the trees, and a sense of unease ran coldly through his veins. It was not another gift, not an offering he would want to see. His fingers curled into his palm, but there was naught he could do. It was too late to act.

A string of pixies fluttered through the trees, broken and scattered in their rush. Behind them followed a half dozen high fey towing a parcel netted by spellwoven twine. The parcel's size was troubling enough, but Liana's unspoken warning made it worse. Veil purposefully uncurled his fingers, brushing them over the wing of the fey who rested at his feet. It would not do to let on that any of it was worrisome. Let them think their fey lord was only at play.

By the time the procession had made its way to the dais, half the crowd had given their notice.

The front and foremost of the messengers bowed deeply. "A gift from the elven lord."

"How enchanting," Veil purred. "She does *so* continue to make sheep's eyes at me." There was a rumble of laughter through the crowd, and Veil considered playing it off, demurring to open the parcel later. But far too many had eyes on it, and the shape of the thing was too obvious for minor deceit. He ran his fingers absently over the wing that brushed his thigh, the fey at Veil's feet having shifted to see better. The rest were drawing nearer, their interest not easily lured away.

If he attempted to ignore the presentation with the audience's attention on him, it would seem like cowardice and fear.

He straightened, gesturing widely with a hand. "Let us have it then, this gift from the halfling lord." The words tasted bitter in his mouth, but he'd not much choice in saying them.

The parcel had been laid on the steps of his dais, and the fey who had delivered it let their gazes pass over it before finally bending to remove its shroud. The air filled with the sudden tang of herbs, elven magic, and tonics unfamiliar. A breeze rose, mild enough to avoid notice had it not been scented with cardamom and flowering lianas. Veil resisted the urge to press his eyes closed.

One by one, the layers of the shroud were removed, leaving a single transparent cloth over the thin gray form that had once been fey. There were no murmurs of the deadening coming from the crowd, only silence and stillness. But Veil could feel it, the strange emptiness like a hollow. Like barren ground.

It tasted of the foul magic of the elf lord's Second, and Veil disliked that most of all.

He stared down at the body, the shell of a one-time nymph. She was gone, her energy not returned to the earth. Events had escalated, whether those present were aware or not. It was no longer merely the deadening of the land. It was costing his fey their lives.

The elven lord had forced his hand and outed their secret. Veil drew a breath through his nose, ready to make a pronouncement about the ill-timed presentation.

Then a call echoed through the forest. It immediately and irrevocably piqued the interest and perked the ears of the sea of fey. Veil let a wicked smile crawl across his lips at the realization of that call, a warning, report from his warriors that a spellcaster had been found.

He stood to face the crowd, saved by the reprieve. "The fates have brought us an offering of their own this summer night, a rare treat that has not been matched in many seasons." Each turned to him with eager expressions, attention rapt. It was what they lived for. It was what they craved.

Veil's chest swelled, and he raised his arms, his words met with a raucous cheer and unfettered screams when he announced, "A hunt!"

15

FREY

After a signal toward the castle and the following succession of calls that warned the sentries of what I was about to do, I fell back into the mind of the dragon, holding it steady. A thrill ran through me again at the ease of the action, and I nodded once toward Steed.

Willa spun, her short sword drawn to cut free the spelled bindings that held down the creature's wings. Each of the guard had exchanged their long weapons and loose clothes for short, slim gear. The dragon's claws were as long as a man's legs, its entire body covered with spikes. It was not a beast one would want to get tangled up with.

Steed took his dagger to the twine at the dragon's shoulder, warily eying the beast's massive head. He gave me a long look once he was done, and I returned it with a smile. "All of them," I told him, not wanting the beast tied, even the mouth that could breathe fire and the tail with its deadly barbs.

Willa swung along the creature's body, climbing onto a scaly knee to reach the bindings over its wing. On the other side, Barris and Merek worked in tandem, and I had to hold the beast still to keep its reflex from stretching its leathery wings. With a thought, I lowered the beast's snout, allowing Steed easy reach. He carefully cut along the armored flesh, Steed's entire body as tall as one of the creature's horns.

When they were finally done, my guard stepped away, and I took one long, steady breath before I urged the beast to spread its wings. The creature stood to its full height, drawing in a breath of its own before its wings came swiftly out and down, brushing the earth and buffeting us with wind. And then the beast, finally looking like the dragon it was, spread its wings wide as they lifted to gain air. There was a heartbeat, and then another downward strike. Junnie gasped beside me, and the dragon rose from the earth before diving right over our heads.

I let out a breathless laugh as the others took cover, their hands over their heads and knees bent. I let my head tilt back to follow its progress, and the beast turned hard before the castle walls, driving up as it went sideways, exposing its belly where I suspected Chevelle was standing. I let it swing wide around the mountain before bringing it near in a slow circle again. My feet were moving, following their path to the castle, to the keep.

I had to stop to close my eyes when the dragon neared its perch, to direct it in without seeing through my own eyes instead. When I did, I was startled by how massive he seemed inside the keep that I'd inspected only days before. The beast settled between the towering wide stone columns that were like windows overlooking the mountain below. I bade him to stay while I made my way up the castle steps and had to bite down my grin at the soldiers and sentries who stood in the courtyards and pathways, still and staring skyward.

It was a long walk from the path where we'd met the others and the height of the keep, but the dragon waited, satisfied with my command. It was not what I expected, and I wondered if the same would hold true when he was well rested and not worn down by the journey they'd just put him through.

I came through the stone doorway slowly, watching the beast's massive form rise and fall in the steady rhythm of his breath. He was watching me, but in the shadows, he was so unlike the beast we'd met below. In the dark of night, he would be darker still, his scales only reflecting the glint of moon or torchlight and nothing else. He would be a lethal hunter, even without his deadly fire. But he did have that, and as I stepped closer, I smelled the sulfur of it and felt the strange sense of electricity in the air, which reminded me of the way it felt after Anvil used his talent.

I remembered the talk of dragons from when I was a child, stories of how they would roll on the ground, scratching their backs and necks against the nearest rock, avalanching stone down the mountainside or snapping off trees that were too spare to hold the weight. When I had traveled with Asher, I'd seen patches of scorched earth and heard tales of animals that had been taken and homes that had been crushed. They were not cruel animals. It was just that they were so large and hungry.

"There," I murmured to the beast. "We've no interest in causing you pain. I only want to feel your magic and to understand why the fey have sent you away."

The dragon stared watchfully back at me. He'd no idea what I was saying, but his gaze belied that fact. I moved closer, willing him to remain still. Part of me wanted to glance over my shoulder to be certain no one was watching—Chevelle would have my head if he witnessed what I was about to do. I half smiled at the thought, but it fell away with a breath when

I took another step and felt the heat of the dragon's exhalation.

I reached a hand out slowly and steadily and stared up into the eyes of the massive beast. Even with his snout nearly touching the stone floor of the keep, his head still towered over me. A large tooth jutted over his lip, and a nervous chill went through me. I eased closer, placing my palm flat onto the warm, dry scales of his snout. He let me, because I had hold of him, but a purr and the chuff of warm air came from his nostrils as he regarded me.

"Yes," I whispered. "The worst of it is over. We'll do you no harm."

The dragon's inner lid scraped horizontally across his eye as he watched me. It was a long moment before his massive head finally shifted as he moved to rest it on one of his massive forelegs. His claws slid across the stone floor, his gaze still distrustful.

It would take time. I knew that. I only hoped time was something we had.

~

IN THE DINING HALL, Merek regaled Junnie, Ivy, and Aster with tales of the dragon's capture as Anvil and Thea looked on. Barris sat at the end of the table, his freshly bandaged arm resting tightly against his side as Willa curled fire over a short blade again and again, apparently attempting to teach him a new skill. They didn't seem to notice my entry, and when Merek proclaimed that he had single-handedly scaled the dragon's back to secure the creature's neck, Thea rolled her eyes and shook her head.

There were fresh stitches down Anvil's forearm and a bright-pink burn peeking out of Merek's collar. I hoped it was worth it. I hoped the risk I forced them to undertake would gain us ground.

I glanced up to find Chevelle by the far wall, watching me. From his expression, I could only assume he saw my guilt and doubt. I straightened, taking a long breath before walking to the table.

Merek fell silent, his boisterous tale going flat at either my apparent mood or my station.

"Junnie," I said. "Will you be staying on? I'd like to share what information we're able to gather with you."

Her mouth turned down. "I would greatly appreciate that, but I'm afraid you'll have to send a missive. There are a few leads I need to follow up on before they run cold." She gave me a soft smile. "It is the summer festival, after all. I hear this one is going to be quite a show."

"Quite," I said, thinking of how Veil and the attending fey might have responded to my well-timed gift.

"I've left what information I could with Rhys and Rider, and I will return as soon as time permits."

"Thank you," I told her. "May your pursuit be successful." Her expression said she had every intention of it, and I added, "Please let me know if there is any way we can assist."

Junnie stood to take my hands in hers, squeezing them lightly. "Thank you, my Freya. And may your own task be undertaken well." When she released her grip, she said, "I can check in on Ruby before I go."

"Please." I'd been eager to have someone who had seen her condition from the start look in on her, and with Thea gone, I'd had to trust in other healers and the changeling Liana. It did not sit well with me.

I hesitated before walking her to Ruby's rooms, glancing at the others who'd risked so much. I would reward each of them, but not there. Willa would receive a higher charge. I would have Chevelle do it—the honor would mean more to her coming from him. And Merek was in need of nothing, but we could present him with a horse finer than he could ever trade for, as well as new armor. The others would be harder, but it would be done. I gave them a nod then cast a parting look at Chevelle before walking out with Junnie, Aster, and Ivy on our heels.

In the corridor, Junnie instructed the women to wait with the horses, and I gave a command to a sentry to gather supplies for them. Junnie's dog watched her impatiently, by all appearances ready to go at her side, but she urged the dog to stay with the others, likely because Ruby hated the beasts. All fey hated dogs, but this one was especially offensive, given that he outweighed nearly any fey.

I smirked, giving him a scratch on his massive head. He smiled back at me, his mouth wide and his shaggy hair splayed over a dark-mahogany eye.

I turned, walking with Junnie through the maze of corridors, one goal in mind: figure out how to stop the deadening of the base energy and the filthy spellcasters who had caused it. When we entered Ruby's room, I gestured the sentries who watched over her out. The room smelled of tonics and herbs, evidence the healer had just made her rounds. Junnie showed no sign of reluctance, making straight for the table that made Ruby's bed.

Ruby was silent and still, the only movement a slow rise and fall of her chest. Grey sat in the corner, his constant presence not merely due to his concern for her, but because I'd ordered it. Ruby was the one person with the knowledge the spellcasters needed, and she would not be left alone.

Grey's flesh had lost most of its rawness, the skin healing to a shiny pink with ridges in the worst areas. Ruby's had not been burned. Her mother had been a fire fey, and even though

Ruby was half elf, her skin had been protected. Her injuries were much deeper, her energy exhausted when the changelings had used her as a conduit.

As Junnie's hands ran over Ruby's temples, my thoughts returned to what she'd said in the study and her assumption that the stone Veil had taken was that cursed ruby. The spellcasters didn't need that stone any longer, as they had used Ruby—a powerful fire fey even if she was half elf—to break the darkness of Hollow Forest free.

I could think of no reason that was not tied to this dilemma for Veil to have taken the dragonstone from my jewels, so I'd sent my guard to bring back a dragon to study. I'd not known I would be able to reach the creature's mind, assuming they were too complex, their magic too much like a fey. But the ability had opened possibilities to us, and as soon as the dragon had a moment to rest, I would take Rhys and Rider to study how its energy worked.

I would be able to urge the dragon to use its magic on command.

Junnie's words cut through my ruminations. "She's healed considerably." Junnie glanced at Grey. "When the tonics are removed, does she wake on her own?"

He stood, crossing his hands behind his back. "Not well. She rattles tinctures and recipes and swats at whoever comes near. I'm not sure she truly sees us, but I believe she recognizes that we are here. By touch, if nothing else."

I averted my gaze because I'd witnessed what had given Grey that idea, the way Ruby reacted when he'd held her hand in his and her thumb had crossed the ridges of his scars.

Junnie nodded. "It is good that she's kept at rest a bit longer, then." She met my gaze. "Liana is doing right by her."

"Thank you." My voice sounded more distressed than I'd

intended, but I didn't waste time with regret for it. "And when she does wake?"

"I believe she will be as hale as ever, after a time. The darkness does not change who a person is."

She let her words sit with me, the second reminder in a single day. Junnie knew what was inside of Chevelle. She understood because his work at the battle of Hollow Forest had saved her life. The darkness that was inside of him was what allowed her to live.

That didn't mean any of us liked it.

"Thank you," I said again. "I will…" I took a long breath. "I will discuss it with Chevelle and bring it to Rhys and Rider in the morning."

Junnie nodded. It was the right thing to do, a thing I could no longer avoid. It was not my only secret, and I had wasted enough time trying to hide and not wanting to trust.

"Before you go," I told her, "one more thing."

~

JUNNIE WAS GONE. I'd shown her the manuscript Rhys and Rider had found, the one detailing how Finn and Keaton had gone from ancients to wolves. She'd confirmed what I'd suspected: it appeared as if the key to deciphering those details was on a missing page.

I did not think it was by accident.

I sighed, staring up at the canopy above my bed. The muffled clink of Chevelle removing his armor and then the splash of water in the basin sounded as I took a wide arc around the castle in the mind of my hawk. The grounds were quiet, the dragon sleeping. There was little movement in the courtyards and around the stables, only the normal routines of guards on patrol. I let the bird go, opening my eyes as Chevelle settled beside me on the bed.

He faced away from me as he unlaced his shirt. I did not look forward to what might lie beneath, what Veil might have done. "I should have asked Junnie for something," I said, but he only shook his head. Neither of us wanted to regale Junnie with the tale of a fey lord intruding into our bedroom. It was embarrassing and infuriating that Veil had succeeded in doing so more than once.

The torchlights flickered out as Chevelle turned to me, lifting the shirt carefully over his head. His shoulder was outlined by the spare moonlight coming through the window, and I did not argue to see what damage Veil had managed. Chevelle's fingers brushed the bare skin of my arm as he lay beside me, trailing a hand up to cup my cheek. He leaned in, placed a kiss soft on my lips, and then braced his head on his arm to look at me.

He could see better in the dark than me. I didn't think that would ever stop being annoying. "Are you smiling right now?" I asked.

His laugh was soft. "Not at all." His thumb pulled at my scowl.

I gave it a little bite. "Junnie wants us to tell Rhys and Rider," I said.

I thought I made out the movement of his smile falling. "Yes," he answered. "It's going to have to be now." He twined the fingers of his free hand through mine. It was easier for him to let go than me. It always had been. Everything connected to Asher felt terrifying to surrender. I'd spent so many years keeping it hidden to keep us alive, but that was over.

Chevelle had the connection to the darkness required for casting, and the secret that Asher and Chevelle's father had experimented, long before Isa or me, felt so dark. It was that which had given Chevelle his connection, the ability to move power for stronger spellcasting. Asher had tried to force him to use it, as had Chevelle's own father, and keeping it hidden was all that had kept Chevelle alive. He had lost so much because of it—his mother, for one—but had he revealed the ability, Asher would have taken much, much more.

My mother's whispered words from so long ago came to me: "Light magic excels at growing, dark at killing things." Her fingers had played over my hair in their constant battle to get an intricate braid to stay. I had thought she was telling me stories, explaining the power the elders refused to detail. "Fey magic is the energy that flows between." I could feel the echo of her touch, the memories less painful since her tormentor had been laid to rest. But there was something my mother did not say, something we had learned the hard way.

Spellcasting was none of those things. Spellcasting was subverting energy from its natural course, stealing it, something only a being like Asher would do. Asher had tried to root his ideology within the son of his head guard. Asher had cast upon Sapphire when she'd been with child, and when Chevelle had come out a disappointment and his mother was marred by it to a mild degree, she had been quietly banished. Her namesake eyes had gone that stranger shade of blue, bits of her flesh scarred so that she kept them hidden beneath elaborate gowns. Chevelle's father, Rune, had been a part of it, I was certain—even if I had not been witness to the actual event. And when I had tried to escape from beneath Asher's thumb, Sapphire had been delivered to the castle gates, those eyes that had been a mirror of Chevelle's cleaved from their sockets as a warning, a punishment.

We had stayed to prevent Asher from doing harm to everyone he touched. And though none of us knew it, he and

Rune had tried again with other beings, with humans, fey, and who-knew-who else. Asher had made a deal with the spellcasters who'd brought the darkness onto fey lands. He had found a way to place the connection into Chevelle, and he had unleashed that power into treacherous hands.

The magic used for spellcasting was a dark, malevolent thing, but in the manner Asher had used it, it was especially vile.

Chevelle brushed a thumb over my knuckle. He hadn't known how his connection worked when he was a child, but he would have understood the need to hide his ability without even the constant warnings from his mother. As such, he'd been unable to use it, to practice and learn. When it had finally slipped free of him, bad things had happened. He had kept it bound within him since, kept it safe and secret until Asher had used his own casting against me.

Until Asher and the Council stole my mind.

Then Chevelle learned the ways in which it was used and had to discover how those methods applied to his own to unbind me. But he'd never gotten that far. There were limits. There were dangers.

It was apparent he was still learning. I had not been keeping track exactly how much, but it was the only way he could have been able to stand a chance against a fey lord. I didn't know how much of that was because Veil had been wounded by a poisoned blade or because we'd taken on the darkness in the fires of Hollow Forest. And it was true that off of fey lands, Veil could not access the base energy. But Chevelle had outmaneuvered him. He was getting stronger. It was how he had saved Junnie.

I tightened my grip in his. Junnie was a creature of the light—it was the only energy she could reach. She could not have saved herself against a spell that powerful. "Council broke into Asher's vaults," I said. My voice was hushed, but speaking of the attack seemed loud in the darkness of our room. It was not so long ago that we saw burning pages, the broken block, the scattering of scrolls, the crunch of the Council leader's bones as I broke him in two. "Do you think they knew of this then? That they were searching for his casting ledgers because they understood what was happening with the fey?"

Chevelle moved closer, bringing our hands against his chest. "No. They were here to destroy. Had they known, they would have waited."

I wasn't sure that was true. Their goal had been to destroy the North and its rule, yes, but that ruler had been Asher, and his rule had been spreading.

"In the morning," Chevelle said, placing a gentle kiss on the tip of my nose. "All of it can wait."

"All of it?" I asked.

I could hear the smile in his voice when he said, "Well, not all of it."

I waited in the darkness, thinking he would speak of sweeter things. He let me wait. It was no secret I had trouble keeping patient.

When he finally spoke, the words made me laugh. "Let's talk about this dragon."

16

VEIL

THEY RACED THROUGH THE TREES, STAYING LOW BENEATH THE canopy as they drew from the river of energy within the earth. The thrill of the hunt had roused even those who had been torpid with drink, but their echoed crashing through the forest—behind the more driven mass of the high fey court— would do nothing to dissuade their course. If the noise of the horde alerted their prey, then the chase would only become that much more interesting.

They had found one of the spellcasters, but their thirst had not been sated. They'd roamed the forest en masse and had picked up the trail of more.

Veil drew in a long breath of the forest air, searching for the scent of those who had gone before them. The pursuit had picked up speed after the calls coming from ahead had shifted their direction toward the elven lands.

The spellcasters were making their way toward the boundary. They would know it was their only chance for escape once they heard the calls themselves. Most fey were capable of crossing the ancient boundaries, but that did not mean it was without risk. The energy it took to cross would be lost to them until their return. One would be unable to replenish without coming back onto fey lands. It was, after all, why the spellcasters were trying to break free of those bonds. The deadening that had taken the forest nymph whose body lay at the foot of Veil's dais would be coming for the rest of them soon. The source of energy that fed them all would run dry.

Veil pinned his wings against his back and dove toward the earth, a mass of high fey swift on his tail. He swerved smoothly past a tree, adjusting his path to follow the calls of the watchmen ahead. There was a hiss of sound behind him from a tracker who'd caught the new scent on the wind. The stench was dark and sulfurous, a warning that the spellcasters were busy laying more traps.

Veil gestured at his warriors, and a line of them flew wide. He heard eager cries behind him and felt his chest swell with pride. They were nearing the boundary of stones and flowing water, and his fey had a taste for blood. The anticipation was rapturous in itself, but finally getting hold of the beings who had allied with his betrayers—who had caused peril to all fey lands—was going to bring far more pleasure than the chase alone.

As they closed in on the border between fey and elven lands, the mass that followed Veil spread to plot their course. Whatever plans they had devised, the spellcasters would stand no chance of getting out alive. As long as they were caught before crossing that boundary, he would have them in his trembling hands. He would devour them, drawing their energy free until nothing was left but the ash of their filthy castings.

A sharp yip echoed through the thinning forest, followed

by a long and doleful cry. It was the howl of an ancient being bound inside the hide of a wolf.

Finn and Keaton were at the elven boundary.

17

FREY

At dawn, Chevelle and I dressed in leather armor, forgoing as much metal as possible to avoid interfering with the energy of the dragon. We walked the corridor in silence, the halls hosting a few spare guards while the fey were occupied with their summer festival. When we entered Anvil's study, Rhys and Rider were already waiting.

"Good morning, Lord Freya," Rider said in greeting as Rhys inclined his head.

I gestured them both to sit but remained standing myself.

I took a long breath. I needed to get the secret out and be done with it before I convinced myself to postpone things further. Chevelle stood beside me, as calm and steady as ever.

"I spoke with Junnie before she left," I said. "She does recognize some of the script in the work you found in Asher's study, but she's afraid the page that holds its key is missing." The brothers nodded, apparently unsurprised. "She's promised to look into the document's other notes when she returns to the village and its library vaults." She would investigate what was left of them after my aunt's rampage, anyway. I cleared my throat. "I know you've spent a great many hours studying in our own libraries to discover the key to fey energy and how the deadening of it might be stopped. I'm afraid I've withheld information that may be of help to you."

Rhys and Rider were still, but their gazes betrayed a spark of interest.

"You know that the crossing of magic does not work, that the children created between too-different energies will not survive. The energies are incompatible, and when thrown together, they become too volatile." I shifted, resting my hand on the hilt of my sword. "Volatile" was not the most precise word, because what happened was always entirely predictable: someone would die. Rider's dark eyes stayed on mine. "The exception to this rule were Asher's children, and a single half-fey girl. Ruby's mother was strong and clever, but no doubt her tactics were bought from the same source as Asher's and paid in blood. Those children were brought into being not in a natural manner, but by the hand of a powerful spellcaster."

The torches along the wall were lit, and the tall windows of the study cast the light of a hazy dawn across the room's ancient furnishings. It did not make me feel less cold. "It was not only our survival he guided. As his talent progressed, he was able to give Isa the ability of my mother's family line, to spell into a being of dark magic that which has only been found among the light." That much they already knew.

I pressed on. "We"—I glanced at Chevelle. "Those of us who were aware of Asher's misconduct were mistaken in thinking he only dabbled in corrupt magic, in assuming that it was not a more thorough occupation."

Chevelle's gaze strayed in my direction, but he did not look at me. I would not argue terms with him. Even if the darkness was inside of both of us, it didn't make it less malignant. I went on.

"In the years before Asher's other children—his experiments with fey and human hosts—my grandfather took to toying with those nearer to him. With the dark elves he held within his rule." Rider's shoulders straightened slightly, his eyes going to the fidgeting of my hand, a contrast to the stillness of Chevelle's beside me. I continued, "In addition to keeping me alive when the energy of my parents could not join, he cast onto the child of his head guard, and in doing so brought harm upon both the child and the mother. By some miracle, both survived, but the child bore a connection to the darkness Asher used in the casting of that spell."

Rhys leaned forward, his gaze moving slowly to Chevelle. Both brothers had evidently suspected. But they would have, I supposed, because they had seen Chevelle cast. Chevelle and I shared a bond different from the brothers but no less powerful. I wondered if Rhys and Rider had been able to sense the way the power moved between us.

"As such," I explained, "that child, Chevelle, is able now to... *divert* the energy needed for casting to use at his will." When Chevelle frowned, I added, "To an extent, at least."

The brothers were quiet for a long moment before Rider asked, "So your talent is not that of a conduit? You are able to give direction to that energy?"

"And when you say 'divert,'" Rhys asked, "do you mean temporarily, or is this only a single direction, a route away with no return?"

"It is something I am still coming to understand myself." Chevelle's voice was smooth and steady, though my fingers still trembled against the metal of my sword. He glanced at Rider. "It is not unlike a conduit, but I am able to direct it with the aid of words and powders. I'm not certain the volatility of it on its own."

My stomach dipped. It was what spellcasting had always

been. It was dangerous, capable of taking on a life of its own. It was why the binding words were needed. It was why no one with a bit of sense dabbled in it. Chevelle was lucky to be alive after what Asher had done.

He looked to Rhys. "And yes, it does seem that I may only aim its intent. I've thus far been unable to return the energy to any form other than its initial strike. I lose my grip on it once it is discharged." Chevelle's brow drew down. "Though that may be only that I'm not strong enough to hold on or demand its return."

"Unlike the fey lord," Rider said. "He is able to release that energy from within himself, but he seems able to both draw it in and release it back to its original form."

They carried on for a moment while I swallowed my misgivings and pressed down my own energy, which felt as if it could fight back. My palms went slick with sweat, my mouth dry. I drew a long breath through my nose.

The room had gone quiet, the three of them watching me, waiting.

"Yes," I said. "And so"—I cleared my throat once more—"we do have some inclination as to how the spellcasters' magic works, even if we cannot determine why it has brought on this deadening or if that is even what is at fault."

Chevelle's eyes were on mine, fixed and settled, and I took another deep breath. "When Veil stole the dragonstone from my jewels, I sent the others to bring one of the creatures to us so that we might study the way the fey energy moves through it."

Rider nodded.

I dragged my sweaty hand over the hem of my shirt. "The fey energy is resistant to metal and to running water, among other things, so we would do best to avoid those where we can. There are nymphs who thrive in still water ponds, but the streams create some sort of interference. Metal, however, will cause a greater disturbance and inflict pain."

Rhys and Rider stood, removing what ornaments they could from their own uniforms. They did not seem anxious, but I couldn't say whether it was owing to bravery or something else.

The ice lands were populated with creatures far larger and more dangerous than our own. The vicious spikes and deadly flames might intimidate the rest of us, but when one had been up against a beast three times the dragon's size, with razor talons and spitting flesh-melting venom, our creature might not have had the same effect.

The brothers dropped the last of their metal onto the table and nodded, ready to depart.

I gave them a short nod in return. "To the top of the keep."

~

I FELT for the dragon's mind, as I'd done nearly constantly since the creature's arrival, and found it sleepily watching birds in the light of the early dawn. As we made our way to the top of the keep, the dragon seemed to sense us, rousing from that relaxed state into something more aware. I held him fast, but I wondered if he would truly attack us otherwise. I wished I'd paid more attention to my studies from long before, because dragon lore tended toward repeating the most out-of-the-ordinary tales, not their normal habits and tendencies. I quickened my pace, and none of my guard challenged the decision that I go up first.

We climbed the last few steps as the keep opened to the sky in a wide platform of dark stone, a few wide columns, and very little else. As a child, I had wondered at its purpose, but once the idea of bringing a dragon back to the castle arose, so did my memories of the scars among the stone beneath my feet. Long grooves cut into the floor, weathered with age. The dragons had once lived among the fey, sourcing their energy from those lands, but that did not mean they had been held within the ancients' boundaries.

It was those boundaries of woven spellwork, metal, and running water that kept the fey mostly on their own lands. But the dragons were not tied in the same way as the fey, and airborne creatures who did not need to recharge the energy inside themselves for decades at a time were undeterred by such protections.

I drew in a long breath of the cool morning air, unable to keep a smile from crawling across my lips. There, sitting steadily and waiting for our action, was a creature who hadn't been seen near the Northern territory in years. I reached out with my mind, feeling the low and heavy pulse of energy that lived within him.

I had never before been in the mind of an animal who held magic. I had never felt another being's power so intimately, but the thought brought me up short as I glanced at Chevelle. He watched the dragon with a hand on his waist, where there waited no sword.

"It's safe," I told the others. "Just stay clear of his snout."

The dragon's sulfurous breath was scalding, but nothing else without its fire. I would hold it steady. I would have the creature within my control despite the intimidating size of his body and his power. I was smaller, but I was not weaker.

Rhys and Rider walked around me toward the dragon, and Chevelle stepped forward at my side. "I can feel his energy," I said. "There is so much about him that is unexpected."

Chevelle was silent, a steady presence as I studied the being on the other side of the connection. It was warm and dense and not like anything I'd touched before. My voice was quiet, but Rhys and Rider were close enough to hear. "Veil's energy feels warm to me, but there is a lightness to it I do not feel here. Veil's seems softer, more pliable, and capable of an easier flow."

Rider looked back at me, his examination of the creature's dark scales paused. "I cannot feel it. There is nothing here that feels tangible, though I imagine I would be able to sense it during a strike."

I laughed. "Probably not something we should try just yet."

Rider smiled. "And what of our energy?" He gestured between himself and his brother. "What does it feel like to you?"

I drew my brows together. "Cold, or at least cool. I might have once said a bit dead, but there's something…" I frowned, unable to bring it to mind. "I'm not certain. Your connection is different than Chevelle's and mine, but so is that energy. It's hard to pin down."

Chevelle's voice was low. "And what of mine?"

"I don't have anything to compare it with. Our bond has been in place for so long, and it's not as if I can reach anyone else in the same way." I shook my head. "I can't put it into words."

"Try."

I sighed. "Warm, I guess. But not torrid in the way of the fey. Tingly at its edges." At his raised brow, I added, "Darker. Deeper, somehow." He nodded, and I asked, "What does mine feel like to you?"

He opened his mouth for an instant then quickly pressed his lips together again. I wasn't certain whether he didn't want to discuss our bond in front of the others, or if he didn't want to discuss the energy that Asher had spelled into me. I realized I didn't truly want to discuss either matter.

The power I'd had before was manageable, even as heir to

the throne. But what Asher had thrust upon me tended more toward an uncontrollable trembling of earth and stones, the foundations of everything. It was not the same as what had been spelled into Chevelle. His magic was separate from that darkness, the murky thing that was his connection to the energy required for spellcasting.

He was nothing like the fey. Veil's energy swelled up from beneath the earth, a fountain of warmth rising through him and into his command. It was not like the elves, either, neither light nor dark.

"It's that conduit that the spellcasters are after," I said, "that connection to the base energy they cannot reach on their own."

Rider nodded. "Asher's castings upon those children did not work in every case. Only the strongest bloodlines survived, and even then, their magic was volatile."

A chill wind cut across the platform, hitting my face and tugging at the length of my cape. I did not want to think of the boy who could pull silver from the air or the cackle of the fey who'd rained ice upon us from his place in the sky. Those threats were gone. "So we find the connection, and we figure out a way to cut it off. We sever it or block it however we can."

Rhys and Rider stepped back, allowing me space to maneuver the dragon as I saw fit. I did not know precisely how its energy worked, so I supposed it would be best to test it outside our small circle to prevent any accidents.

I closed my eyes, feeling myself fall deep into the dragon in a way that was not possible with other beasts. He rose to his full height, stretching his wings up and out, pressing his claws to the stones of the top of the keep. The creature rolled his head, snapped his jaw, then pushed off in a slow and solid wingbeat that thrust a gust of air across us. I opened my eyes to watch him sail off the central tower and swoop low over the castle walls before swinging wide. I took him down the hillside, just far enough that we could see him clearly over the walls. I had been afraid of losing him with distance, but I had yet to feel even a strain on our connection.

I glanced at the others beside me, who stood in a line, watching the beast. I closed my eyes to sink fully into the dragon's mind, feeling out the connections to the animal's power. It was a sleepy sort of thing, deeply hidden and slow to respond. Dragons didn't need their energy for daily life. They had wings to fly and fire to fight and teeth to cut and tear. Dragons were capable of flight faster than even the fey, but this one's magic felt ancient and lumbering.

The creature seemed so near, already so familiar. I wondered if that connection could be strengthened even further over time, the way it had with my birds. I felt Chevelle's hand on my back and realized how far I'd slipped away. I let him steady me and reached again for the energy inside the dragon. Heavy as it was, I was able to call it to rise, slow and dreamlike, and when I released it into the atmosphere, the rocks around the creature split into broken halves with an echoing *crack*.

I opened my eyes, staring not through those of the dragon at the pieces of rock severed in two, but through my own, at a massive scaled creature, spiked and dark and so in its element among those broken stones.

I frowned. The thought was strange, but not inaccurate. The dragon did seem more fit to life among the dark rock of the mountain than in the thick fey forests.

"What's wrong?" Chevelle asked.

His words brought me back to the present, and I turned. "Nothing. It worked far better than I expected."

His expression was solemn. "Do you think you can prevent

him from cracking the stones of the keep, or should we try this from out there?"

I chuckled. "Afraid I'll drop us through a dozen levels?"

He did not laugh, and I recalled nearly losing Ruby through the practice room floors with my new, unwieldy powers, and Chevelle falling through the shattered glass floor of Veil's home.

"It's fine," I promised of the dragon. "I have him."

And I did. Once the dragon was back on the keep, I held him there and used trace amounts of magic so that Rhys and Rider could attempt to examine how it worked. But it was not the brothers who had drawn the magic free, and once I'd felt the energy move, sensed its flow and the impression it left, I could not deny its similarities to the movement of other energies I'd felt in the past.

"I think..." I shook my head, unsure exactly what it was that I was thinking, unable to bring it from that realization into words. "I believe I can feel the warmth of it. And in doing so, the utter contradiction that is the feel of a human."

Rhys and Rider straightened where they'd been kneeling near the dragon, their gazes going into sharp focus at my expression.

I swallowed. "It's a sort of hollowness within the humans. That must be... Well, it feels like that emptiness must be where the deadening comes from."

Chevelle's voice was quiet beside me, his frame too still. "You're certain that it is something inside them that's the cause?"

I bit my lip and thought about the few humans I'd been exposed to before Veil had taken me to the encroachment. I thought about the feel of one, a solitary being, and the way that directing even a single human drove knives of pain through my skull. And I had been unable to stay near the seething mass of humans that had waited beyond the barrier of fey lands, even without reaching out with my power.

I sighed. "I've no idea what Asher spelled into me. There's no way to know that's not what's making me..." My words trailed off because I wasn't entirely certain what I felt.

Chevelle stepped closer. "He did not spell this into you. This is a pure gift from your mother's line."

I nodded even though I was unconvinced. We would never truly know what all Asher had set into motion, what other darkness he'd set free.

Chevelle stared at me. "I know. I would feel it."

The tightness in my chest eased, if just a bit. Chevelle was right. He would know if my gift wasn't pure because of the magic Asher had spelled into him.

The dragon was resting, so I slipped back into its mind. I might never have used my gift on a magical creature before, but I had felt my own magic. I had felt Chevelle's. I understood that what Asher had spelled into me was different, and that was separate from my own natural skill.

I had met the sensation of the dragon's ponderous energy with those expectations already in place. What I felt when I returned to the creature was so outside of those expectations that I gasped.

The others surrounded me instantly, Rhys and Rider searching out an unseen enemy, but Chevelle's attention only on my face. "What is it?" he asked.

"He's reaching for the source. I can feel it." I shook my head in disbelief. "He can access the base energy even from here."

18

VEIL

V<small>EIL AND HIS COURT FELL UPON THE ANCIENT BOUNDARY</small> dividing fey and elven lands just as the spellcasters they'd been chasing drew up short, but it was not the magic of the boundary that had stopped the spellcasters. It was the head of the light elves and her Council guard waiting on the other side.

Juniper Fountain, daughter of Elerias and adversary to all things fey, stood front and center, her crown of braid and gilt robes shining brightly in the late-day sun. The magic inside of her was radiant, and though Veil could not reach it with his own power, he could feel how it touched the flora around them. Beside her was a line of golden-haired warriors, women and men with hard expressions and ready bows. Veil flew into the clearing with his wings spread, unable to bite back the smile from the thrill that was a fey hunt. He let his gaze roam the line of the elven guards then inclined his head toward Junnie at her ferocious stroke—flanking her and that guard was a string of wolves that stretched from tree line to tree line on either side.

Junnie did not spare Veil more than a glance. Her bow was drawn, and what was surely a poison-tipped arrow was aimed right at the scattered mass of spellcasters between elf and fey.

Veil let his gaze fall onto their prey. The smattering of trapped changelings stared back, some at the horde of eager fey, some at the line of wolves and light elves. Veil recognized a few of the changeling's faces, but even as he watched, their shapes flickered in and out of form, dancing between what their magic could hold and what their spelled traps were drawing from that energy. He wondered if the spellcasters had succeeded in their attempts at Hollow Forest and whether they had created a channel so that they might devour more energy from the source.

He wondered how fast that energy could be replenished. He wondered if this battle would be as satisfying as the last.

Veil's booted feet touched down on the well-worn ground before the boundary, his silken shirt long since torn away in the ravaging of the hunt. His chest was bare, and the sun was warm upon his amber skin, the wind light against his feathered wings. He felt alive with energy and anticipation, intoxicated by the power of it.

"Your time has come," he told the changelings before him. His voice was nearly a purr, his eagerness plain. Behind him, a wild cackle rose, then a groan of pleasure and the murmur of assent. Veil wet his bottom lip. It was swollen and tasted of blood. "This day, you will pay for your crimes against the fey. You who are so low as to not even warrant the trials of court, the play of the fates. Before the sun falls, your time will end."

He let his smile make the promise that it would not be pleasant, that the changeling fey responsible for the deadening of the land would not be allowed to pass their energy back into the source.

They would not be allowed to have any single say in the matter, even if they were to spell the words to life.

Two wolves moved forward, not wild beasts but the ancients Finn and Keaton. Their eyes were on the fey lord, watching. Veil had never known the twins in life, but he had heard the legends. He knew that Freya could not reach these creatures because they were more elf than beast. He knew that Junnie could. She could not read them directly, though, because although her connection to canines was strong, none of Elerias's line could touch the minds of other elves. The power needed to transcend the elven form, to fall into something *other,* was difficult to grasp even for Veil. But he understood that he had felt something similar.

The thought had him glancing down his fey line, meeting momentarily the gaze of Liana. Her skin had shaded to a cool steel gray, and Veil had the unpleasant realization—somehow, he kept letting it fall from his mind—that she was also a changeling.

He stared back at the spellcasters, the mass of changelings giving everything they had not to show their fear, not to invite the horde upon them. Veil's eyes rose again to Junnie across the boundary.

"You will have them," he said, "as soon as we are done."

Despite his promise, the corner of her mouth turned down, and she loosed her arrow. It flew straight and true and into the heart of a changeling fey at the center of the group. A dozen more arrows took flight, and the field erupted into chaos and smoke. Blackness and sulfurous ash exploded through the air, the wild calls of fey met with the silence of the waiting elves on the other side. Between them launched a multitude of spells and traps, each tied to the dark energy that could sap all that was inside the fey.

The thrill of the hunt crested and sang through Veil's blood. He pulled the energy deep inside himself and strode forward with a grin.

19

FREY

Rhys and Rider had returned to the study to research their ideas after we'd spent time examining the energy of the dragon. Chevelle and I sat alone in our rooms, having a private dinner while we contemplated what we'd learned. The deadening of the fey magic would have a disastrous effect on all kinds if it kept spreading, and as much as I didn't want to, it seemed the only way to fight it was going to require us to use the same malevolent methods the spellcasters had used. I worried what risks we would take that were impossible for us to see, what might happen once we unleashed our own magic to fight the spread.

I bit into an apple, thinking about how Junnie had refused the fruit earlier. The light elves created something soft and sweet, so unlike the bitter tang in the varieties grown in Camber. It was not simply our magic—every part of our tastes and customs differed. And yet, all of us would suffer at the hands of the cursed plague. It would happen whether the starving fey were allowed onto our lands or not. The humans had affected the magic at the boundary, which meant it was likely that the deadening could affect elven magic as well, even if we didn't know how.

I set the apple down, the outline of my bite mark etched into its flesh. It so reminded me of Ruby and the way her teeth would leave those sharp, jagged lines and the way the fruit became discolored from her venom.

Chevelle slid the apple out of my sight and gave me a look.

"Right," I told him. "I'll find something productive to do."

His lip quirked as he went back to whatever he was scribbling onto parchment. I closed my eyes to the scratch of his quill, finding the dragon with my mind.

The dragon was there, waiting not for me, I thought, but for the coming night. The sun was not yet low in the sky, so I urged him to take a sweep of the castle grounds. I could have used my bird, but I wanted to test our connection more. Since we'd had a chance to study his magic, it would be safer for me to fly the beast farther out, to risk that I might lose him beyond reach. It did not feel as if I could.

The dragon soared over the mountain, high enough to not cause alarm but low enough that I was able to take in the features I'd grown so accustomed to seeing from the eyes of my hawk. We roamed in large, slow circles, widening the range to a distance I'd not been able to reach with other creatures. My hawk had been with me since I was a child, and my connection to her was the strongest I'd ever felt. I'd been able to find her far down the mountain, even when I'd been bound.

The dragon was different—he had magic. It was ancient and more connected to whatever the talent was that ran through my line. And he was fast. The dragon was so massive and his wings so swift that when pressed, the ground passed beneath us with near-dizzying speed. Soon, we were soaring over Camber, over the town that spread through the dark mountain rocks scattered with thin budding trees.

Summer had come. The fey festival had likely already drawn to an end. I thought of Veil, imagining his words when he would next see me. *I received your gift*, he would say with that displeased set of his jaw.

I let myself wonder if he'd been able to hold his expression and what the reaction had been from the gathered crowd. And then, because I could not seem to stop myself, I urged the dragon forward, toward the boundary between elven and fey lands.

I would not cross it. I didn't believe it was capable of severing the link between me and the dragon—my fear stemmed more from what they might do to the returned beast. They had chased the dragons off for a reason.

The thought brought me up short, because Veil surely knew I would realize the dragonstone he'd taken was missing. Certainly, it had not been a clue. I shook off the idea, diving harder into the dragon's flight. It would be dark soon, and I did not want to fly too near fey lands after sunset with the dragon.

There was a low grass clearing where the mountain valleyed off toward the flatter, forest-covered lands. A river cut through, and some of that water had been diverted by the ancients to create the boundary after the fey wars. It had been a punishment as well as protection, and the spells remained in place, secured by the ancients Finn and Keaton.

As we neared the clearing before the boundary, a cloud of dark smoke came into view. It was widening as we drew nearer, filling the sky with something that was not the hazy gray of fire smoke but a darkness like the night sky.

The black of spellcasting.

We dove toward the site, and a broken assembly of figures came into view. A low mass of shifting shapes leapt back and forth through the stream, over rocks, and into and out of the vapor. Wolves. So many wolves. A line of Council guards stood steady, their arms raised with bows, their golden hair and gilt robes shining in the late-day sun. Beyond them, across the border and past the cloud of darkness, was a chaotic mob of fey.

I bit back a hateful curse.

The dragon's wings drew hard against its body, propelling the beast toward the fight. I felt no fear or hesitance from the dragon, and though I did not want to risk the animal, I could do nothing else with the danger below. I had to save Junnie.

VEIL

THE VISCOUS CLOUD OF DARKENED ASH BILLOWED AND SWELLED, moving around the spellcasters as protection from both elf and fey. It would not hold, Veil knew, but he could not say how many would be lost before the energy of the changelings was diminished enough to bring them down. The shush of an arrow barely missing his ear brought his attention from the cloud of darkness to the telltale markers of a different sort of threat. A shadow crossed the ground, the attention of the fey around him drawn to the sky.

The shadow moved closer with unexpected speed and size, its shape jumping and morphing as it crossed brush and stone. Veil let his gaze find the dark mass overhead, and could swear the beast looked him straight in the eye.

Veil cursed.

The dragon roared.

Fire erupted on the boundary.

Veil leapt into the air, not to meet the newcomer but to gain distance from its deadly fire. Below him, fey screamed, but it was hard to tell whether it was the cry of battle or nearness to the burning, pleasure or pain. Above him, the dragon blew past, its trail of flame colliding with spellcast smoke. Waves of noxious flames, painful and acidic, washed through the air, and Veil flew higher, gasping in search of a clean breath. His gaze followed the dragon's path, where it rose over the trees just shy of fey lands, turning back to come at the spellcast cloud once more.

When Veil saw it again, there was no doubt. The creature's glare cut into him, the thing's eyes glowing red and holding what felt like a promise. Veil did not back away.

The dragon made another pass, lower to the ground but no less violent. The creature did not seem to care for those near the fight who might be burned, but Veil supposed that was because it understood that unlike the fey, the elves were a safe distance away. He supposed it had not a thing to do with the actual dragon, but with the elven lord who watched from within.

He swung back toward his people, calling them away to wait for the next pass. The dragon fire was quelling the smoke, even if it had not dissipated enough to reach the changelings inside. She may have acted heedless of those scattered near the spellcasters, but the dark lord Freya was giving them the chance they needed to fight the source of the spells before more fey were lost.

The dragon sped low once more, its wings shoving down in a massive press of air as its fire collided with the smoke. When it rose again, it released an earsplitting screech that tore through the field, causing even Veil to wince at the nearness of the sound. The dragon rolled through the sky, a trail of smoke hovering after its long, spiked tail. The fey around Veil rushed forward again at the receding smoke and ash. A body fell through the haze, the shaft of an ironwood arrow protruding from its back. The figure shifted, its flesh sliding free of the arrow and reshaping in less than a breath.

But the changeling's tactic was too late to save it. A dozen fey fell upon it, tearing the body into ragged bits with magic and claws. Veil glanced again down the line. Liana stood barefoot at the edge of the stream, in quiet contemplation of the cloud as a battle raged around her. She seemed to draw a long breath, raising her head to the sky to track the dragon before kneeling to the earth. Her gown was ripped and torn, her skin the color of a midday storm.

The elves on the opposite side of the barrier drew together, edging back as water rose within the stream. The trickle became a torrent, the widening path of that water pushing toward the changeling fey. Veil drew his own power in, collecting it with the gathering of the source within him, waiting and watching—doing everything his instincts rebelled against. His warriors prowled before the cloud of smoke, hungering for spellcasters to emerge. Wind and rain and hail pierced the shape, but very little made it through to their target. A pile of shattered ice lay scattered on the earth, unmelted in the warm air, leaves and vines tangled through broken stone.

The dragon returned, its massive claws nearly dragging the earth even as they were drawn against its ribs. Its jaw opened wide in a scream, and then fire spilled onto the earth and ash. A hiss of steam rose from the widening flood brought by the elves, the heat of fire and water and acidic smoke stinging Veil's skin. He drew his wings tighter to his back, leaping forward just as his fey did the same. Liana's fingers sunk deep into the earth, the elven guard loosed their arrows, and his own warriors walked into fire.

There was a sudden shudder of the earth as tall, thin spikes of blackness rose like blades from the ground beneath their feet. Cries of pain rent the air, and blood spattered onto Veil's outstretched hands. He threw the strike he'd intended to save, despite not being near enough his target. It was time to break these vile changelings before one more of his kind was laid to waste.

His power slammed into the cloud at the same moment the dragon drove through again. But it was not only the heat of flame that tore into the spellcast smoke. It was ancient magic, warm and deliberate, an energy Veil had not felt since he had been young.

It was the dragon.

Veil worked his jaw, tasting blood, and pressed harder with his own energy. The cloud fell into mist, an ashy haze that struggled to regain roots. The shadowed figures of the changeling fey—the spellcasters—came into view. Beneath the changelings' feet, the earth was a viscous pool of black, the remnants of their waning spell that would burn through weapon and flesh.

Junnie raised her arm, her guard drawing up and into formation, ready to shoot, to fight. The floodwater split as a wave of writhing fur and sharpened fangs rushed forward, the wolves' bodies rolling and thrashing as they drove in a mass over the boundary toward the spellcasters.

The fey beside Veil flinched as if wanting to retreat but unable to show fear. They watched in apparent horror as the wolves—at the hands of a single light elf—tore limbs asunder. A horrific sound rose through the clearing as the collective whine of those beasts joined with the dying screams the changelings had spelled to life. Veil's stomach turned. He did not look away.

Junnie's guard loosed their arrows, striking true in their targets and missing every wolf. Missing even the watching fey.

Junnie too did not look away, though her eyes held more satisfaction than Veil thought could be seen in his.

The dragon shrieked, rising high above the melee in a darkening sky. After it was done, when the final mist had settled and the last spellcaster was no more, Junnie called the wolves back to her own land. The water rose to brush against the remains of the spellcast blackness, hissing and purring before it fell again away. The land was washed clean where Junnie stood, but the fey side was nothing but blood and ash, littered with the bodies of his own kind. Junnie let her gaze stay on Veil a moment longer, her men tending to the wounded animals with the care they might show their own.

She wanted him to see that she'd betrayed her own laws—or maybe that she'd written new ones—in order to see her vengeance through.

He didn't think he liked the taste it left in his mouth, though that might just have been the blood and the ash.

Liana was suddenly beside him, standing silently as she watched the light elves move away, apparently unstirred by the slaughter of so many of her kind and unaffected by the battle they'd just waged. Her skin was dark and bruise-like, the color vague and unsettling, though Veil thought that, too, might have just been the blood and the ash.

1

FREY

I drew back from the fight, from the mind of the dragon, to the flicker of torchlight and the shock of nothing happening, aside from the steady scratch of quill on paper. Energy pulsed through me, my body charged and mind alight. My shoulders rose and fell with breath, the bewildering change to stillness and near silence overwhelming. I let out a huff of air, and the noise seemed deafening.

Chevelle glanced up at me.

My mouth popped open, but I couldn't quite get words to come.

"Is something amiss?" he asked, as if maybe I'd seen a shifty figure at the gate or some guard not doing their duties.

I heard myself laugh.

Chevelle set down his quill.

I was suddenly grinning, a wild and dangerous emotion thrilling through me. This did not seem an assurance to him. I pressed a hand to my chest, heart hammering beneath my palm but no longer due to the stress of the fight. Then I remembered I'd abandoned the dragon. I shook my head, closing my eyes to drop back into the mind of the beast. To my surprise, he had not flown south or toward his home. He was heading in our direction, as if he had intended to return to the castle. I decided to let him go for a bit to see if I was right.

When I opened my eyes again, Chevelle had moved closer. His expression was grave.

I took hold of his hand. "The spellcasters are dead." His brows knit, so I explained, "Junnie and the fey at the border. I saw it through the dragon."

He looked at me strangely for a moment, likely owing to the distance of the border, then let go a long breath. I could not help the grin that returned to my face. For so long, I had struggled with the issue of whether to stay in the castle as lord or to go out and help our people. I had just won a way in which I could do both, a way in which the distance could be conquered.

And we had killed the spellcasters. The force behind the deadening was no more.

We only needed to stop the darkness they'd left behind. I shoved to standing, tottering as I rose too close to Chevelle. He steadied me with a hand on my arm and with a look.

"To the study," I said. "We need to tell the others."

~

LIANA RETURNED FROM THE FIGHT—TO our castle and not to her own kind—in the dark of night. She'd left the blood and ash covering her skin, partially bared by what appeared to be a torn sapphire gown. It was difficult to be certain of the color, as filthy as the fabric was. She'd walked right through the front gates, letting all who wished witness her pageant, along with those who had no interest. When she was met with the head of the guard, she requested an audience with the Lord of the North.

"Shall I bring her to the throne room?" Kieran asked when word finally reached us.

I shook my head. "The study is fine." She'd practically lived in the castle for weeks, making herself so at home that before she'd left for the festival, she'd ordered our seamstress to cut her a gown. I didn't know why suddenly she'd decided to approach her visits as formal, but I could only assume it was owing to my business with Veil.

I glanced at Chevelle, who was already fastening his sword belt. I shoved a dagger into my own but did little else in the way of arming my person. I did not trust Liana, but I was not afraid of her physically. The changeling's magic was nowhere near as dangerous as her maneuvering.

When we entered the corridor, we were met with Dree's approach, her agile hands carrying an array of wine. "Leave it in our room," I told her. "We won't be long." The corner of her mouth twitched, and I wondered if the entire castle staff had heard of my dealings with the fey.

A look passed between Chevelle and the guards at the end of the corridor, one I presumed meant *stand at the door until our return*. He'd been exceptionally watchful since Veil's last intrusion.

Steed, Anvil, Rhys, and Rider were still in the study from our earlier meeting, and they glanced up, eyes narrowing at our entrance.

"Liana," I explained, frowning because the single word was enough to encompass all the visit might entail.

Steed and Anvil were mostly healed from their journey to

retrieve the dragon, though I noticed Steed had not pushed up his shirtsleeves until after I had gone. A thin red line, criss-crossed with even stitching, ran over his forearm. When he caught my eyes on it, he gave me a look. I threw him one right back.

Chevelle cleared his throat. "Liana will know more about the spellcasters' magic than she will let on. We need to do what we can to gain that information."

Rhys and Rider nodded. Anvil only scratched his chin. I was with Anvil—it was likely Liana would give us no more than what she already intended.

I sighed, taking a chair at the head of the table while Chevelle positioned himself near the window, where he stood with a hand on his sword. I remembered the last bargain we'd made with Liana, trading the diary in exchange for her hold over Chevelle. I'd never figured out exactly what the changeling had wanted with him, but as I thought of it in this new light, with the manuscripts and documents scattered over the long table describing ancient magic and the weaving of spells, a sick sort of feeling rose in my stomach.

Chevelle did not meet my gaze. His eyes were on the door, and I followed them to find the changeling fey.

"We see you," I snapped at her display. "Feel free to change into something less filthy."

Liana smiled, showing too many too-straight teeth. "No need to put on airs," she said.

I watched her move leisurely into the room, wondering if her current appearance was entirely for show. Maybe the battle had stolen the last of her energy, and she was unable to shift further. It seemed unlikely. The battle had been on fey ground.

She stopped before me, and I had the feeling she was annoyed that I hadn't made more ceremony of her arrival.

"What is it?" I asked.

She inclined her head slightly, bringing a fisted hand up for offer. At my look, she shifted a brow then turned her hand over and opened the fist. Resting on the changeling's palm was a dragonstone. My dragonstone.

My gaze snapped back to hers, my emotions flashing between anger and confusion. "What is this?"

"A gift from the lord of the high fey court."

It was not a gift. The stone was mine. So it was something else, but I didn't know if it was another clue or more maneuvering.

"The spellcasters are dead," Liana said, "but you know that." She shifted her hand closer, urging me to take the stone. "Now, your bargain must be upheld. The price for your halfling's release must be paid."

I kept my eyes on Liana as I reached for the stone. It was dark and sharp and strangely warm against her hand.

It was not that the stone was overly warm. It was that Liana's flesh had been cool. The idea snagged my thoughts, wanting attention, but the dragonstone wanted it more.

The stone waited in my palm, heavy with familiar energy. Small as it was, the dragonstone was ancient, and within it lay a power that felt as strong as my brushes with some of the worst of the high fey. My eyes shot back to Liana's.

She purred.

"Veil gifted me a stone with fey energy."

"Yes," she said. "It's the only proper way to keep a dragonstone. I don't know why you'd have one any other way." Her dark eyes floated to Rhys and Rider. "It will need to be fitted within her staff."

I clenched my jaw to prevent my mouth from dropping open. I wanted to ask why Veil would gift me something that would give me such control over my powers. But I remembered how the other stone had busted and the way I'd used the staff in our battle at Hollow Forest. My stomach dropped. "He wants me to use it to fulfill my bargain."

"Of course," Liana said flatly. She brushed her palms together. "Now, let's go. It's time to wake the halfling."

22

RUBY

RUBY SMELLED SOMETHING SHARP AND SWEET A MOMENT before searing fire shot through her veins. She leapt to her feet, boots knocking glass vials from the table to shatter on the stone floor. She shook her head, pressing her eyes closed to clear the fog. When she opened them again, she stared down from her perch on the work table to see a changeling fey. *Liana*.

Ruby hissed.

Liana crossed her arms. "Well, that is just entirely lacking the appreciation it ought."

Ruby scanned the other figures in the room: her brother, Steed, shirtsleeves rolled up and arms at the ready near his sides, Chevelle and Anvil, expressions stern but weapons sheathed, and Freya, who had that same stubborn set to her jaw as the first time Ruby had seen her, though her current bearing was nowhere near the awkward and bumbling girl she had once seemed. Freya was Lord of the North, and she looked mad as hell.

"I'm here." The low voice came from behind Ruby, settling her jagged nerves. "You're safe."

Her instinct was to turn and give Grey a look at the latter comment, but she held steady. She did not want to face him in front of so many after the terror of her dreams, after the burning.

"You could have brought her out slowly," Frey snapped at Liana.

The changeling only shrugged. "She doesn't respond the way others do. It's entirely a gamble."

Frey's scowl softened as she turned back to Ruby. "How do you feel?" Sliding a slender hand over the clasp at her vest where the medallion was carved with the hawk and snake of her crest, Frey added, "Aside from disoriented."

Ruby nodded. It was maybe all she could manage at the moment. Frey moved forward with a waterskin, though Steed still looked as if he was ready to trap a wild animal. Ruby took the proffered container with a trembling hand. A strange expression passed over Frey's face as their skin brushed, but whatever it was disappeared in a blink.

Ruby took a long draw from the bag, tasting the spice of warm winter wine. She drew a ragged breath, eyes going to the changeling Liana, who smelled instead of ripe summer fruit. Ruby's lip drew up to bare her teeth.

Liana held her gaze. "It's time."

Time. Time to repay the debt. Time to fulfill a bargain made on Ruby's behalf.

Ruby leapt down from the table, landing between Steed and Frey. "Right," she said. "Next time, don't wait so long to wake me."

She did not want to explain what she'd seen in the darkness and did not want to talk about how she felt. She only wanted this over, done, to be alone with her waking self.

She wanted to let go the rage and fear simmering inside her.

So Ruby did not say another word as she strode from the room. It was time, and Ruby meant to prepare for battle.

23

FREY

"I WANT THREE GUARDS AT HER DOOR," I SNAPPED AT KIERAN, "and seven more at each end of the hall." His brows drew together and I added, "If she leaves, if she goes too silent, if anything at all happens or does not, come here to inform me."

Kieran inclined his head in a sharp nod, then turned and strode from the room. Dree and Ena followed behind him, having settled the last of their trays onto a makeshift table before Ruby. Ruby had left her healing bed and strode directly to the armory, fitting herself in guard-issue clothes and with a bevy of knives. Her red curls were tied tightly into braids at the base of her neck, but she still smelled of herbs from Liana's ministrations. She ripped into another hunk of meat, apparently ravenous. Grey's eyes stayed on me as I blinked at the sight of her devouring half of the display. I shook my head, facing the others with a sigh.

Anvil and Steed leaned against the dark stone wall of the training room, and Chevelle stood nearby. He had not intervened in my orders to surround Liana's room with guards, despite having already given orders himself. None of us wanted the changeling within earshot of the discussion we were about to have.

The light of early dawn began to creep through the high windows. I tapped a finger against my bracer then crossed and uncrossed my arms. "Word from Rhys and Rider?"

Steed nodded toward the door, a tall, carved-wood affair opposite us in the massive open space. The door opened, evidence of both my distraction and the inferior hearing of my blunt human ears.

The brothers strode into the training room, my carved ironwood staff in Rider's hand.

"That was fast," I said, ignoring the look Chevelle gave me because I'd clearly just been impatient for their return.

Rhys inclined his head. "The work on the staff was mostly complete. It was only a matter of adding the stone. Binding it."

As they moved nearer, I had to still the urge to reach for my staff. It was unsettling how I'd grown so attached to it, and I refused to give in, instead curling my fingers into my palms. "Have you tested it?"

Rider chuckled. "We are not so brave."

"Did it bind well?" Chevelle's voice came from beside me. I'd not even heard him move.

I shook my fists loose, wanting to be rid of the tension that was tingling through me.

"It will be fine," Ruby said from my other side.

I startled then rubbed my eyes. I needed to get a hold on my edginess and the energy pushing it.

"It appears to have bound together seamlessly." Rider held the staff aloft, its stone at eye level. It was jagged and dark, very unlike the stone that had been there before.

"If this gets into the wrong hands—"

I cut Ruby off with a look then remembered how long she'd been under. "The spellcasters are dead."

My words were flat, but Ruby only smiled. "That uncomplicates things."

The spellcasters had used Ruby as a conduit at Hollow Forest. I wasn't certain if her concern had been for them doing so again, or only that she'd intended to plot her revenge. I pressed my lips, letting my gaze roam over her pallid face. Liana had done well with keeping her alive, but Ruby still needed time to recover. She'd been unconscious for what felt like ages. "Also," I said, "we have a dragon."

She jerked back just a little, and I had the pleasure of catching her rare surprise. She stared at me. "Why would you not tell me that *first*?"

I chuckled, but when her gaze traveled to her brother, I wondered if she was thinking of his faint pink burns and stitched-up arm. I cleared my throat. "Now that the spellcasters are gone, you are the last in possession of the knowledge used to spell your talent and mine into beings to whom it does not come naturally."

She frowned. Then she waved a hand, her wrists bare of bracelets and baubles. "None of that matters now. We have what we must to heal the land."

I felt my jaw go slack. "Do we?"

She gestured toward the staff in Rider's hand. "The fey lord has gifted you fey energy." Ruby's glittering emerald eyes came back to mine. "And within you are the dark and the light." Her eyes strayed to Chevelle, but the tingling within my palms gave way to a sway, to the sensation of standing in a hard wind that has suddenly ceased.

"Ruby," I breathed, "what are you saying?"

She swallowed, wrapping a hand firmly around my upper arm. "I haven't seen that look on you in a while." Her words fell into muttering as she settled me onto a stool that had been provided by Grey.

Ruby knelt before me, and even though I sat on the stool, she had to look up to face me. "It was why the ruby was so important." Her voice was low, her face solemn. "It was not merely a stone," Ruby said. "The ruby you retrieved from the vault had been spelled by Asher to act as a conduit itself. It may have worked for smaller castings, but he did not have the power to reach that energy in the amount he needed, not in the way—" Her words fell away again, seeming to dry up.

I felt Chevelle and Anvil shift behind me. Grey leaned in to hand Ruby a metal cup. After a long draw, she pressed her fingers across her lips then started again. "They needed a better conduit for what the changelings had in mind. They needed to open a vein into the energy's flow. When they could not manage it with stones, they went for me. It worked."

"How long have you known this?" My voice was strange to my ears, though I wasn't sure what Ruby heard.

Her face pinched. "I knew as soon as Veil and Liana drew me from the darkness—from the fires. When I became that conduit and as they broke me free."

Liana was a changeling. Veil was a fey lord.

I glanced again at the staff held by two elves from the ice lands, the feel of their magic oddly chilly. "Liana," I said. "The moment she touched the staff... When we were attacked in Veil's home and Pitt was taken, she retrieved it for me." I breathed. "Her magic was *cold*. It's been that way ever since. And when Ruby woke, it was as if I could feel it on her skin." Ruby's gaze did not waver. Ruby knew. "You felt like Liana. You felt as if your fire had gone cool."

"I still have my fire," she promised. "I'm still whole."

"Something of Liana's borrowed energy lingered though." My voice remained low, but the strange trembling was gone. The mess my grandfather had started was beginning, finally, to make sense.

"How does Liana reach the energy of the ice lands when no other fey can?" Steed asked.

Ruby stood. "She doesn't feel entirely fey. None of the changelings do. Maybe it has to do with their ability to shift form."

"They think they can break free," I said. "That's why they were trying, because they think if they get free of the base magic, they can reach other energies elsewhere."

"Maybe they could. Or maybe Asher was only risking it to get what he wanted." Ruby shrugged. "Doesn't matter now." She clapped her palms together, and the sound echoed through the room. "Let's try out this staff, shall we?"

Grey gave her a flat look, but Ruby's eyes skirted his face. She'd been avoiding so much as glancing in his direction since she'd woken.

I couldn't help but wonder if I'd been a fool. For far too long, I had heard the elders' warnings that the humans would consume us. As we stood, the humans and however they were tied to the land were eating away at the base magic the fey required to live. And it was coming our way. I had always assumed those warnings referred to me, to the part of myself that was not light or dark, not elven at all. But the warning still echoed, and even as I understood there was far more to the humans than any of us had known, it did not seem so far off that the cautions may have pointed to Asher's larger plan. It would explain why my mother's connection to the humans and my own human heritage terrified the elders. Because we had been under Asher's command.

"If the spellcasters opened the vein at Hollow Forest, then the magic of the source would still be bleeding out," I said.

Chevelle and the others remained at my back, but I let my gaze take in Ruby, Rhys, and Rider, those who had been studying this problem from the start.

"It has to be drawn into use," Ruby answered, "by someone capable of moving it in that capacity."

A powerful spellcaster. Someone like Pitt. Someone like Asher. Cold dread settled in the pit of my stomach.

Ruby's hand shifted to her hip, where her slender fingers curled over the handle of a black-leather whip. "The spellcasters are dead." Her tone said it was over. It said there was no reason to consider what might have happened if the spellcasters had not been caught. She gestured toward the staff. "Now," she said, "let's get this over with so you can introduce me to that dragon."

24

RUBY

"How long are you going to ignore me?" Grey's tone was even and not unkind, but his question was too blunt to disregard entirely.

Ruby frowned, not turning from her task. "Until I'm ready." His answering hum sent a strange feeling through her. She tightened her hands into fists. "Soon. Just let us get through this."

Grey's silence seemed to say the what-ifs she did not have room to think about. *What if we do not get through it? What if there is no more time?* She wanted to turn and glare at him, but she didn't think she could look, because there was a chance those things were not what his expression would say at all. There was a chance she was entirely wrong.

She snapped the chunk of ironwood bark she held into two pieces then ran her blade down the edges to smooth the fray. She shoved the dagger back into its sheath, sliding the ironwood pieces into her belt and grabbing an apple from the table before she spun to follow the others out of the room.

Frey had decided it was not safe to toy with fey energy

inside the castle. "Outside," she'd snapped. "It has to be outside." Ruby was pretty sure Frey was stalling, though everyone could see she was itching to have the staff back in her own hands.

Ruby walked through the arched stone doorway, a place she'd passed countless times when training a bound Frey. The corridor was cool and dark, and when Ruby realized it was too quiet behind her, she stopped and gritted her teeth. She would not look back, not yet. "Are you coming?" she called.

Grey did not answer, but he moved with his signature speed, the heat of his body coming up behind her as quickly as a whip. Her lip trembled with the urge to speak, but she bit down on it, forcing her feet to move instead. They strode through the corridors, pace set to catch the others who'd gone ahead. The castle staff went on about their duties, but Ruby could feel their eyes on her as they passed. Word must not have spread that she'd been awakened, that the last of the Seven had been returned to the high guard.

They rounded the final corner to a long corridor, where Steed leaned casually against the open gate. Early-morning sun filtered through a thick haze outside, and Ruby could just see Anvil and the others making their way across the court-yard beyond. She made the mistake of letting her gaze fall off track, and Steed reached out to snag her wrist. She spun, feeling Grey move past, and Steed grinned as he tossed Ruby's apple, which he'd just stolen from her, into the air before catching it with his free hand.

She couldn't bring herself to glare at him, so she only placed a hand on her hip. "We have a duty to attend."

He held her gaze for a long moment, just looking at her. "Aye." He sighed as if satisfied at his inspection then tugged Ruby close for a quick hug. He was so much bigger than her, and she was lost to the outside world in the cocoon of his embrace. "I wish you'd stop fooling around and risking your life," he whispered. Her heart stuttered, but Steed let her loose and flashed a smile as if he'd said nothing sentimental at all, tossing the apple aloft as he turned to go.

Ruby stared after him as she caught the apple in her trembling hand. Had that hug been one instant longer, it might have torn her apart. But Steed knew her, maybe better than she knew herself.

She slipped the apple into the pouch at her side and followed him over the courtyard stones.

∾

In the center of the open courtyard farthest from the castle walls, Frey stood before each of her Seven and accepted her altered staff. Ruby wasn't certain how the brothers had managed to bind the energies together or if they'd only bound each to the ironwood and the magic inside, but she hoped it would hold. Frey would need to be able to wield her own magic while using the stone to access fey energy. They needed to seal Hollow Forest and create a new boundary to keep the deadening of magic from spreading. Because as much as the fey might enjoy it, no one was going to eradicate the humans on the off chance it might prevent the barren lands from expanding.

Ruby sidled up beside Chevelle, but before she got a word out, he gave her the look. She crossed her arms over the leather chest plate of her uniform. Ruby was tired of that look. She'd seen it the entire time Frey had been bound. It said *don't push her*. It said *she's volatile*. When Frey had been bound, Ruby supposed Chevelle had been right. He was the expert on spell-casting, after all. But Frey's bonds were broken, and even if her mother had gone mad at the hands of Asher's torment, that did not mean the tremors in Frey were going to cause her to crack.

If anything would do it, it would be the overwhelming amount of power that swam through Frey's being. And there was nothing to be done for that.

"So," Ruby said, "what does it feel like?"

Freya turned, her black hair loose in the wind and her dark eyes lit with tension as her fingers flexed around the iron-wood staff. "It feels right."

Ruby grinned. *Right* was the answer they needed.

Frey drew a long breath as if letting the energy roll through her, her gaze never leaving Ruby. "Now," Frey asked, "what's the plan?"

Ruby uncrossed her arms, itching to throw her fire—which she'd not been able to do the entire time she slept. She hoped she hadn't, anyway. She stepped forward. "We go to Hollow Forest to seal off the fissure so that no one can ever access it again."

Frey nodded as if she had confidence in that part, at least.

"We restore the boundary so Finn and Keaton don't have to stay with it, constantly shoring it up with their energy." Ruby strolled around Frey so that her gaze could linger on Chevelle as he watched them both. "And we create a new boundary for the fey lands, where Isa holds the humans at bay."

Ruby's eyes were on Chevelle when Frey asked, "How, precisely, do I build these boundaries?"

Ruby smiled at the head of the high guard.

Rider spoke up from beside Frey. "They will be spellwoven with each of your energies. If we are right, then the construction will prevent the deadening or any other threat from breaking through."

"Will the fey be trapped inside?" Frey's tone sounded more like curiosity than concern.

Rhys answered, "Assuming all goes as planned, no. The fey will be able to come and go as before. The boundary will take no more than the energy required to cross, and the fey will have no access to the base energy once they cross and are off of their own lands."

"Woven," Frey said, "with spells."

Ruby did not have to see Frey's gaze to know where it landed. Chevelle's expression went still. Ruby supposed she'd poked at him enough. "Give the staff a shot," she whispered into Frey's ear.

Frey lifted the staff a hair's breadth from the stone beneath their feet then tapped it gently back to the earth.

The stones rumbled as warmth swelled over Ruby's feet. "Did you mean to do that?" she asked.

Frey chuckled. "I was only making sure I had my own power securely tied." She tilted the staff toward the outer wall.

"Precise," Chevelle reminded her.

Frey nodded once then shot a blast of power toward the block. It exploded a single merlon from the battlement into fragments of ash. The strike was impressive and Frey seemed pleased, but her face fell when a screech echoed off the castle walls. "Oh," she said. "Right." She took another long breath, closed her eyes, and then opened them to smile at Ruby. "I imagine he didn't like that much."

The screech sounded again, and Ruby's gaze found the top of the keep, spotted with haze and shadowed by the early sun. The shadow seemed to shift and grow before the black mass separated from the tower and dove through the haze.

It dropped toward them with startling speed, and Ruby noticed that only she and Frey kept their footing. The dragon swept past them and over the castle wall, whipping its tail in an arc as it circled back once more. A blast of wind from the beast slammed into Ruby, and she laughed, gasping at its size and speed. Frey stood beside her, both of their heads tilted toward the sky, both of their faces split in wide grins. Frey winced, likely because she knew what was coming, and the dragon picked up speed to swing back once again.

Its drive was incredible in its swiftness, and the dragon skidded to the earth before Ruby had the chance to draw in a breath. The beast came to rest only a few arm's lengths before them, its chest heaving as it lifted its head to the sky for another bellowing call.

Everyone in the clearing shrank back at the sound, but Ruby danced to her toes. She leapt forward as the beast settled, and the creature angled its head so that one round eye could take Ruby in. She proffered her hand.

The dragon obliged. It lowered its head, shifting back so that its massive snout was near the ground. Ruby reached for it, and though she could almost hear the warnings Steed and Grey wanted to shout, they apparently managed to hold their tongues. Fat lot of good it would have done them, anyway— Ruby was about to touch a dragon.

She laughed again, her palm brushing the thick scales of its snout, still slick with mist and dew. She moved forward, running her hand along and drawing it back with her fingers clawed. The dragon shoved closer to Ruby, and she climbed onto its snout. There were shouts from the onlookers, but Ruby ignored them.

The dragon puffed out a sulfurous breath, hints of dark smoke rising beside Ruby from nostrils that were as big as she was.

She took both hands down the side of its muzzle, scratching long and hard on either side of the thing's deadly spikes. Ruby slid free while scratching, her feet touching stone as the dragon nudged her to do it again. She giggled, crawling carefully forward as she drew her hip dagger free to the clamoring of her guard below. She flipped the dagger and jammed the hilt of it against the dragon's skin, running the base of the carved wood shaft in a long line. He snorted and chuffed, and when Ruby slid down again to pat the end of his snout, the dragon gave a contented rumble.

Ruby was snatched from the scales and yanked back by the weapons belt across her shoulder. Steed stared down at her, plainly furious, but he stepped back carefully at a muffled shifting behind her. Ruby tilted her head back to see the dragon once more, its own head turned at just the right angle to give Steed a dangerous look with a single dark eye.

Steed went pale, though surely Freya had hold of the dragon, and Ruby patted her brother on the chest. Steed huffed out a breath, but he let Ruby go. She slid toward the dragon again, leaning back against his snout as the creature settled his head.

Ruby reclined against his warmth, crossing her arms over her chest as she smiled at her watching guard. "I like him," she chirped, "very much."

The dragon behind her purred.

25

FREY

I'd sent Liana ahead with word so that Veil would meet us at the boundary. Together, we might all heal the fissure at Hollow Forest. Ruby had insisted we bring along the dragon, despite my concerns about having it so near the fey. "They aren't going to do anything with Veil there," she promised. "Besides, dragons can fight back. There's a reason the fey chased them off instead of killing them."

I supposed she was right, but I didn't need more to worry about, and I'd already gotten attached to the beast. He flew overhead, high in the clouded sky, as I and the seven of my high guard rode through the low grass that led to the boundary between fey and elven lands. Anvil gave me a side-long glance as Steed let out a low whistle at the carnage along what had been the ancient boundary. The demarcation had once been a small ravine of bedrock and running water, but the recent skirmishes had created a wider, more shallow bed of stones with a shallower-still flow of water. The most recent damage had been done by my dragon, evidenced by charred earth and bare trees.

It was noticeably worse on the fey side, where the boundary wasn't merely collapsed. The changelings had snuck captured humans in to test their effect on the ancient magic. The deadening that affected the base energy on fey lands was also capable of altering the age-old protections that no fey had been able to touch. It was time to remedy that, but I did not have confidence in my ability to do so in the way Ruby and the others seemed to.

"We should go to Hollow Forest first." Ruby's eyes were on the sky, not on the shadowy shape of a giant dragon, but the morning sun low on the horizon. None of us wanted to return to Hollow Forest in the dark of night, let alone be anywhere on fey lands. It was treacherous and deadly in the light, but the darkness was when the worst of the fey came out to hunt and play.

"Word will have reached Junnie last evening," Steed said. "We should expect her by midday."

I heard what he did not say, that we would want her there when we created the boundary between the fey and Isa to close off the humans.

Veil and Liana walked from the trees, a dozen of Veil's new guard behind them in armor and helm. Veil was shirtless, his amber wings tucked neatly behind his back, while Liana wore a long white robe, her hair in silver braids around a pale-gray face. The changeling's eyes were as black as ever.

"Protections," Ruby said when the fey drew near.

Veil glanced heavenward. "Are we not beyond this by now?"

Ruby crossed her arms and gave him a look.

He sighed. "Fine. By my word and upon my invitation, I guarantee protection for the elven lord Frey and her Seven by my right as fey lord and so forth and all that such entails." He gestured vaguely with the words, but they would be bind-

146

ing. His gaze met mine. "I offer no such promises for that dragon."

A smile crept across my lips. "*My* dragon. Thanks to you."

"I'll not take credit for your choices, Lord Freya."

He seemed annoyed that I mistook his stealing the dragon-stone as a clue, but if he'd been less vague or perhaps had simply asked for the stone, none of it would have happened. He'd been so worried about giving anything away or showing weakness to his kind. "Regardless," I said, "I do not regret it." The dragon had followed us of its own accord once I'd urged it from the keep. I would let it roam as it pleased unless the fey caused us trouble.

I stepped into the shallow water that moved slowly over the broken stone of the boundary. "Has the changeling filled you in on our plan?"

Veil's jaw tightened almost imperceptibly at my words, though I had no idea why. "Yes," he answered. "Where would you like to start?" His gaze roamed over me, taking in my wardrobe of black leather—aside from a sword, I wore no steel—then over my newly repaired staff.

"Hollow Forest."

He nodded at my pronouncement before gesturing toward the men at his back. "Take them," he ordered. "With haste."

The fey came forward to seize hold of my Seven as a swarm of pixies swelled from the trees toward Liana. The pixies formed a mass around the changeling, and she rose her arms so that they might more easily carry her. Ruby stepped beside me, and two of the high fey guard moved to our backs to take hold of us by our weapons belts. Veil watched us all, waiting until each of us was airborne before taking flight himself. He kicked off the earth, darting upward before spreading his wings wide. He soared beside us, where we hung not unlike carrion from his fey soldiers' grips.

The trees were green and lush, still damp with dew, and the air was warm. We flew over it all at a pace that took my breath and made my eyes water like the chill night winds used to, the ones that would snap at my cloak and whip my hair against my face from my old roof perch atop the castle. The flight of the fey was not as comforting as that long-ago perch, but it would be over soon enough. The burned remains of Hollow Forest came into view, a circle of ash and broken trees, of shattered rocks spanning a chasm that dipped into dark earth.

It was where Ruby had nearly died.

I found her in the sky, tethered as she was beneath a fey guard who was twice her size, the lines of her body built for flying because she was half fey. But Ruby would never know flight the way they did. It was not part of her magic. It was something no one had thought to spell into her, something she could not have naturally won.

Ruby's mother had helped her survive with the dark words of cast spells, but she'd been concerned more with giving the child power, access to the fire that ran through her own veins. She'd wanted to keep Ruby alive, and she'd severed Ruby's ties with the base energy, but Ruby was neither elf nor fey. She was both. She was more.

Before us, two fey descended from the sky to deposit Anvil and Steed onto the broken earth. Behind them, Grey was dropped somewhat less graciously, but he managed to keep his footing. Rhys and Rider were lowered beside me, my boots clattering onto a pile of broken stone, theirs into scattered ash. Chevelle was deposited solidly past Rhys, and Ruby landed in a somersault beyond both. All of us were safe on somewhat-solid ground. The fey who'd delivered us waited behind the group, nearer the trees, and Veil landed on Rider's other side. We watched as the cloud of pixies delivered Liana, mostly because it was difficult to look at anything else. The swarm rose from her gracefully, shifting as one through the sky before dispersing at some unseen cue.

Liana brushed her hands over the material of her robes, though nothing appeared out of place. Her dark eyes roamed our line of six elves, two halfbreeds, and a high fey lord. "Shall we begin?"

Ruby stepped forward, turning to face the rest of us with Liana at her back. "Frey was born with the ability to control both light and dark magic. The staff will allow her also to direct, with Veil's aid, the fey energy within the stone to weave a new boundary. While we are here, she only needs to seal up the fissure, but she will need Veil's assistance in holding back what flows beneath Hollow Forest."

Liana's voice was low, but she made certain the lot of us heard it well enough. "Are we to presume you are the expert of the fey energy, halfling?"

Ruby did not so much as spare her a glance. "Presume all you want, changeling." Ruby's gaze skirted Veil's then bored into mine. "I was in the fire. I understand how the energy flows."

I gave her a small nod, knowing that her look meant that she'd also felt the connection Veil and Liana had with that energy.

Ruby held my gaze as she went on. "Your magic will not allow you to direct energy that is not your own without a conduit. The staff will act as conduit, but only with the aid of Veil can the fey energy be reached and drawn back to the stone. He is to that energy what Chevelle is to the other." I felt my guard go still around me, but Ruby did not waver. "As such, the two are parallels."

As I struggled to grasp what she was telling me, Liana moved too swiftly to stand between Ruby and the rest of us. I followed her gaze to Veil, who did not seem to particularly relish the comparison between him and Chevelle—or maybe it was something more. I opened my mouth to ask Ruby if she'd meant the darkness inside of Chevelle and what would happen when that darkness met the energy that Veil was made of, but a look from Liana cut me short.

A quiet whisper brushed my ear, a sound spelled to life in only the way a spellcaster could, and my heart went cold. The words she'd given me were meant for no one else. I felt myself moving backward, but the broken stone shifted loosely beneath my boot. "I can't—" I shook my head, moving my eyes from Liana to Veil.

The fey lord's face was hard, his jaw set and his mouth in a thin line. It said that he'd not wanted Liana to reveal what he must know she had. It said that he'd made up his mind.

"No," I told them. "There's got to be another way."

But my words were binding. The bargain I'd made echoed back at me. *Whatever it takes.* I looked to Liana helplessly, but she remained steady. She'd made her bargains. She'd chosen her side.

My blood, of both the light and the dark, ran cold. Within me was something else, too, a bond that connected me—my energy—to Chevelle and to the darkness that was spellcasting. They were asking me to use that connection to heal their land, using Veil as a conduit. But I would be connecting his energy not to that of my ancestors, but to the darkness that was deadening the land. It was more than dangerous to the fey lord. It would end him.

They'd clearly known all along. Liana understood how the fey energy worked. She'd been drawing it for ages, and she'd stood by Veil to help pull Ruby from Hollow Forest. I couldn't understand why they had not simply admitted he was at our mercy, but it was bigger than that. The fey could not show fear—a fey lord could never reveal defeat. But this was not about his position. It was a sacrifice to save his people.

I swallowed the words that wanted to come. Veil and Liana obviously knew everything and understood what he was giving up. They were going to use my connection to Chevelle to drive fey energy into that darkness and destroy it at the source.

Liana's words from the battle with Pitt came back to me, her warning that only the fey lord could direct the river of energy beneath Hollow Forest, along with Ruby's words, that Chevelle and Veil were parallels. Liana and Veil would have laid everything into place: his successor, his plan for the fey. We had come to a place where Veil had to give up his life in order to save his kind.

"There has to be another answer." My words sounded hollow, echoing off the broken stone. No one offered a reply. A pixie flitted into the clearing, dancing through the still air and over the chasm, the pit that was once Hollow Forest. I glanced at the way the sun flashed through the flip of its wings and caught sight of the shift of a shadow behind Veil. An ochre-skinned soldier in armor and helm crept behind the fey lord.

My mouth opened to scream at the same moment the blade pierced Veil's side.

26

FREY

Veil roared, and the field around him shifted into action. His wings burst wide as he spun, his teeth bared and hands clawed in anger or pain.

"Now!" Liana screamed, and for one moment, I had no idea what she meant or who the command had been aimed for. Then the soldier who had stabbed Veil in the side was knocked backward, his helmet thrown from his face to reveal the dark, depthless eyes of a changeling fey.

Liana was on me, her long fingers wrapped about my shoulders to turn me from the scene and toward the chasm that had been Hollow Forest. "Now!" she said again.

"Are you mad?"

"He's been stabbed," Liana hissed. "If you don't do it now, you might lose your chance."

Her words sent ice through me, but even if part of me understood she was correct, I could not do what they wanted. Chevelle was suddenly beside us, shouting commands and throwing his hands with a deftness that confused me more, at least until I smelled the sulfur of that darkness, the rising

153

stench of spellcast energy stronger than any I'd ever felt before. The dragon's screech tore through the air, and Liana was moving me to run with Chevelle.

There had been a changeling hiding among Veil's guard. A changeling and a spellcaster. He had driven a knife through Veil's side.

"Do it!" Liana commanded. "Close the well of energy before it is too late."

I shook my head frantically, and my gaze found Chevelle. His expression said everything. My Second, my anchor, had no hope.

Veil cursed in the melee behind us, the sound rising over the clamor of clashing swords. It was more than that battle, and it was more than a simple changeling hiding among the fey. If Veil failed, the changelings would win far more than a simple struggle or a fey crown. My grip tightened around the carved ironwood shaft of the staff, the cooling hum of its presence suddenly overtaken by the warmth of fey energy. The power in the stone was rising, swelling to meet the connection I'd made with Chevelle.

He stood before me, throwing powders and rushing out words, but he too must have felt the brush of fey powers. His head snapped toward me, eyes sharp. I knew what he would see in mine: fear. Uncertainty. Hopelessness.

"I have to do this," I told him. "I have to end the deadening, and I need your help."

Chevelle swung to face me, his expression hard. "What have they told you?" His gaze flicked to Liana accusingly.

"Now," she hissed again. "We've no time to argue." Her hands were slick with blood, though I'd no idea whose.

I had to stay on task, to focus on the energies rushing through me. "Veil's energy can be drawn through this stone, should he will it. They want us to douse the darkness, to end it before it can spread farther."

Chevelle shook his head. "You've no idea how vast that energy is. There's no way he can—" Then Chevelle's blue eyes flicked to Liana's, realization clearly dawning that Veil was not meant to make it out alive.

"We have no more time," Liana told him.

"You knew all along."

The changeling did not defend herself against Chevelle's accusation.

"And now you risk it all," Chevelle said in a level tone.

Liana's chin came forward a fraction, but she spelled no further words to life.

Chevelle's mouth was hard when he turned back to me. "You know it will kill him."

I swallowed. "It is either him or all of the fey." It was even worse than that, because if the fey lost their access to the base energy, if the darkness spread, we would all be in peril.

Chevelle gave me a long look before he bent to a knee before me. He placed a hand to the earth and took hold of my waist with the other. The fighting behind us faded to a dull thrum as power welled inside me. Bodies moved past us, fighting and falling and flying as the rumble of broken and shifting stones rose through the clearing.

Ruby had explained how the weaving would work, but she did not tell me how I might hold myself together. She did not know how the power and the weaving would affect me. My limbs felt light, prickly, and barely there in the overwhelming presence of power gathered in my chest. The heat in my palm was searing, the stone sending too much power through me, an energy too strong and too strange to control.

I tried to force it back into the staff, to use Chevelle as my anchor and let the dragonstone be the conduit to send the energies toward the fissure beneath the chasm of darkness. But it was drowning me. It was too much, too immense. Through the haze of sound and pressure, the fey lord came into view. He was being helped, carried beneath his shoulders by Anvil and Grey as blood spilled from the wound in his abdomen. Anvil's side was soaked with the fey lord's blood, my guard's sword nowhere to be seen. Grey slid from beneath Veil's arm, whose wing seemed to be hanging at an off angle. The fey lord did not look at me. He only pressed a hand to his side as he was lowered to the ground. When he was settled, I felt the warmth rise even more before it focused into a pinpoint of fiery heat.

Blistering, tortuous pain seared my palm, and I screamed, feeling as if the energy trapped in that staff and its stone might explode and take the entirety of Hollow Forest with it.

Then Liana's cool and slender fingers brushed my flesh, her whispered words cutting through the madness of what we were doing. "Focus," she purred. "Weave."

I gritted my teeth against the pain, staring hard into the chasm of darkness before us all. But we were too late. From the pit of broken earth rose four spires of darkness, ghastly shapes that shifted from smoke into oily spikes of arms, blades, and wings. Nightmare raptors of spellcast darkness welled up from the thing that was the antithesis of the source, the pit that wanted to devour the fey energy. Liana's grip tightened on my arms, her words still and steady, though no part of her could have possibly been calm.

The spellcast beasts rose higher, their ashen forms splitting from the tendrils of darkness rising from the chasm below. Their sharpened wings drove upward, and then the beasts broke free to dive toward the fey lord. Veil attempted to rise to his feet with Grey and Anvil scrambling for weapons as Rhys and Rider lunged forward. The fey lord stumbled, scattering loose rock into the chasm, falling at the ledge with his wings crumpled beneath him and covered in ash. His hands, thick with blood, slid across his bared flesh as the darkness ascended. The spellcast beings speared into him, their sharpened wings and claws tearing new wounds even as the lot of my guard and Veil's own fought them off.

The energy that ran through me slipped backward, spreading sharply and violently into my form. I threw my head back and shrieked, the dragon roaring with me, and Chevelle's hand slipped from my waist. Liana dragged me backward, away from the spellcast beasts, and I drove the dragon toward them with no capacity for an order more than *kill*. Chevelle threw something dark toward the figures, his gaze desperate as it met mine. The fey lord called out, and it was not the cry of victory. Veil's control slipped further, and the energy inside me felt as if it would burn through my very soul.

"I can't," I managed in a broken whimper.

Liana wrapped her arms tightly around my chest, as if she could hold me together by sheer force, as if her changeling form could protect me from the spellcast beasts and the energy breaking me from within.

Chevelle's eyes closed, his chest rising and falling in a long breath. When his eyes opened again, they flashed with something dangerous.

I tried to croak out a *no*, but my voice was gone. Veil was covered in blood, my guard in smoke and ash. The dragon's claws tore into a nightmarish figure, ripping it from the fray into the chasm beyond, but the bird only shifted to smoke and ash, reforming around the dragon's wings in tendrils of slick darkness. The dragon screamed. Ruby's whip snapped. Anvil's lightning cracked. Then Chevelle drove his hands through the shattered rock and into the earth below.

The rumbling of power beneath us rose to deafening thunder, spreading from the land at our feet through the forest bordering the chasm. Trees shuddered before falling from view, apparently sliding into the darkness of the widening pit. I fell to my knees before Chevelle, dragging Liana with me as she tried to hold on to my trembling form.

Chevelle's face was distorted in pain, with blood and ash smeared from his dark hair over his temple. I couldn't know what he was seeing behind his blank gaze, but it was not focused on me or our surroundings. His eyes had gone as black as pitch.

"Chevelle—" My voice broke off in a painful cough, and Liana's arms tightened around me, keeping me back from Chevelle. Keeping me safe.

With his arms covered in ash and his fingers in the dark earth, Chevelle spoke words I'd never heard in a tone that was not his own.

I gasped in a breath and choked on a sob, but the changeling only held me tighter. "Still," she whispered. "Steady."

You knew all along. Chevelle's words echoed through my broken thoughts, my own power wanting to tear free of me but tied to the staff and its stone, to the relentless ocean of power and the clash and pull of energy to energy.

Chevelle had the ability to reach the darkness. He always had. He had thrust his hands into the earth of Hollow Forest. He was going to attempt to direct the fey energy into that endless darkness. Veil had known. Liana had known. They'd brought us there to end the deadening one way or another.

I pressed my eyes closed, my mind brushing the fear of the dragon as it struggled against the spellcast beast that had wrapped around its wings, my power fighting to gain any sort of control or release, to end the state it could not settle into.

The energies of each of us were not interchangeable. But I was of both light and dark, and I was connected to Chevelle through our bond. Veil intended sacrifice, and Chevelle was diving into a darkness that none of us truly understood.

None of us but him. I bit down hard on the pain lancing through me, tasting blood and ash and the hopelessness of regret, then reached out to Chevelle via that connection between us. It felt as if his presence had been stolen, as if he'd been swallowed by the empty hollowness of the chasm beyond. It was the darkness, the energy that was spellcasting, that felt to my own power like a void. And it was terrifying.

I pushed forward with every fiber of my being, with conviction I had no right to have. Chevelle's power took hold of me, and with it, the unstable, unbearable feeling that I might lose control. A sound escaped me, and Liana whispered words to which I could afford no attention. The rush of power filled every part of me, leaving no space for understanding, for any action other than one: to reach the darkness and heal the fissure.

It felt as if I might be torn apart, as if I'd made the entirely wrong decision, but I bore down, pushing harder into our connection. Something in the darkness that had pressed against me shifted, and I remembered Chevelle was a conduit. He could direct it.

The mass of darkness, the thing that felt like energy to Chevelle and the changelings but like a void to Veil and me, fell back, suddenly and sharply. I sucked in a ragged breath, finally able to draw air, finally getting a sliver of relief from the pain, and realized what Chevelle had done. My eyes flashed open to find him, his face turned upward and twisted in agony. We could not fight the darkness. It was too immense. He'd only pushed it back. He was holding it there until I could use the energy gifted by Veil into the dragonstone to weave with my own. I had to create a seal that would prevent what the spellcasters had broken free from escaping.

My face was wet with tears or blood, my eyes matted with ash, but I rose to my knees and gripped hold of Liana, jerking her loose to stamp my staff onto stone. With a deafening crack, the energy poured from the stone toward the fissure the changelings had made. I wove the energies together, but the attempt felt crude and clumsy. I tightened and pulled, drawing from my own energies and from Veil's through the stone. When the patch was nearly complete, Chevelle's hold on the darkness broke free to slam against the boundary like the sea to shore.

It held.

I collapsed.

~

AFTER A TIME, Liana rolled me over, staring down at me with an expression I could not quite decipher. I looked for Chevelle, finding him on his knees across the broken stone, his gaze on mine. His eyes were no longer black. Behind him, Anvil sliced a borrowed sword through a changeling's chest, and the fey fell backward off the ledge. Over the chasm, the last of the spellcast beasts faded into ash, its smoky figure blowing away in a quiet breeze as the dragon struggled then landed ungracefully in a heaving mass on the edge of the chasm and among broken trees.

My Seven stood scattered, their armor filthy and tattered, scouring the ground and the trees for further threat. The last of the changelings were gone. Ruby systematically rolled her whip into a coil, her red braids caked with ash. Grey's eyes were on her, his fingers trembling and bloody. Between them, the fey lord lay on his back, shirtless and beaten.

Veil glanced down at the blood pouring between his fingers, his skin pale yellow around the wound. Then his dull amber gaze met mine. "You are a dangerous being to have around, Lord Freya." His breath came out in a wheeze, his hair matted to his temples. "I do not think I care for it much."

And then the lord of the high court, head of the kingdom of all fey, passed out cold.

Liana growled, gave the lot of us what was almost certainly a frown, then ordered Veil's men to move him into the trees and build a temporary shelter in the woods.

"Will he be all right?" I croaked.

She nodded, kneeling to hand me a scrap of fabric as her dark gaze went to Chevelle. "Veil will recover."

My Second had saved the fey lord. I'd not anticipated anything of the sort. I let my eyes linger on Chevelle. His shoulders still heaved with ragged breaths, his fingers stained dark with earth and spells. I wondered if he could recover. I wondered if he would ever be the same.

27

FREY

RUBY TENDED THE WOUNDS OF THE SEVEN WHILE LIANA FUSSED over Veil and his men. After Chevelle had gained enough strength to do so, he'd moved to my side, managing an awkward shuffle before settling in with a wince. He took the cloth Liana had gifted me and dabbed it with oils before wiping the ash from my eyes. His touch was careful, his fingers shaky, and between the ash and the exhaustion, my eyes ran with tears.

"Have we done it?" I whispered.

His gaze met mine, the only thing steady between us. He nodded once, his jaw tight with what was probably lingering pain. One side of his face was smeared with darkness, his ear caked with ash.

I had known Chevelle since he was a boy. Our bond was unbroken, our trust in each other the only thing that had ever felt sure. "Did you know for certain?" Before he'd made the attempt to hold back the darkness, I meant. Before he'd risked himself to the energy of it and of the fey.

He sighed, his gaze floating momentarily toward the

others before coming back to me. "You asked me how your energy felt, what it was like for me." His hands settled between us, the ashen rag loose in his fingers, dark with soil. I reached for them, letting my fingers twine with his. His voice was low. "It's so strong it's nearly overwhelming. As if it could drown me." He swallowed, not breaking eye contact. "And yet, my own energy urges me toward it. To plunge heedlessly into that sea of power."

That was what the darkness was. That was why it scared me.

Chevelle had known that Veil would be killed. He'd known, too, that the darkness would not be sated. After I'd felt it, even I could sense that much. It could not be sated because it was endless and unquenchable. There was no method to destroy it, only to cage it and never let it free.

I tightened my grip in his, letting my cleared gaze trail again over the chaos of the broken forest as a light wind rustled the leaves. Anvil and Steed shared a canteen, spilling water into their hands and splashing the dust from their faces. Rhys and Rider were gathering the guard's discarded weapons, swords and knives that had been thrown asunder in the chaos of the storm clinking heavily into a pile. Near the edge of the trees, Ruby sat with Grey, patting tonic over the bare skin of his arm. He tried to bat away her ministrations, but she persisted until he wrapped a hand at the base of her neck, forcing her to look at him. For one long moment, Ruby did, and then she closed her eyes and Grey pulled her closer, pressing his forehead against hers in a gesture that was somehow more intimate than a kiss.

I looked away, my stomach turning at what had nearly happened and how close we'd come to losing everything again. Chevelle tugged my hand, and when I glanced at him, his expression was clear. "This was not a failure, Freya. This was triumph against unbeatable odds."

I flinched but forced my lips into a small smile. It was not my victory to claim. It was my Second, the Seven. It was all of us as one.

$$\approx$$

WE LEFT Liana with Veil in the shade beneath the canopy, in what was left of the forest that edged the chasm of broken stone. She had assured us that Veil would be well, and we wanted to reach the boundary before nightfall. We rode at a relentless pace through the thick trees of the fey forests, Veil's guard racing ahead to clear the way. I wasn't certain any high fey would attempt to stop us, as the deadening would come for them if we were not able to put an end to its spread, but Veil had promised us his protection, and his guards had sworn to uphold his word.

We neared the barren ground later than expected, and a pack of restless wolves met us where the fey lands ended. Before we reached the settlement and Isa, the Council sentries called from the trees.

Their Council head was coming to greet us.

The wolves danced, bounding through the narrow trees, their dark fur flashing between the shadow and light. Dry brush crackled beneath our horses' hooves, and when Junnie finally came into view, we drew our procession to a stop.

Her expression was bright. Any worry she might have had apparently fled at the sight of us well. Her cheeks were flushed from running to meet us, her hair bound in tight clean braids. Junnie's robe swept around her as her step faltered when she came near enough to get a look at our faces, still streaked with blood and ash. Her gaze traveled over our tattered armor, lingering on Chevelle's darkened hands. Her flush paled.

Junnie's eyes came back to mine, her worry evident.

"The fissure at Hollow Forest has been sealed," I said. "The changelings—the spellcasters—are dead."

The line of her mouth hardened, and Junnie came forward to help me from my horse. "Who needs tending?"

"Ruby has seen to us." I let my hand linger in Junnie's longer than was necessary after she helped me down. I let her see the promise in my eyes.

She gave me a curt nod and squeezed my hand. "The horses, then." She snapped a gesture at her sentries, and they took to the horses as my Seven managed to fall into an orderly line. Steed leaned heavily on one leg, Anvil seeming to favor an arm.

"We've done it," I said. "Once we've had a chance to weave the magics, the boundary here and the boundary between lands will be secure enough to withstand what comes."

Junnie's seemed to flinch, but it was so small I wasn't certain I'd seen it. I wiped a dirty hand across my eyes.

"Come," Junnie told us. "Let's get you washed and fed."

Our pace was slow without the horses, and by the time we made it to the settlement, Junnie's men had set up wash basins and food. We accepted the offerings gratefully, and as the water was replenished, I took note of the newly channeled stream that cut across the land. My gaze, clear again, came to Junnie.

She gave me a tight smile. "Taking precautions."

I glanced beyond her, toward the makeshift huts and sturdier structures of the settlement. Dark smoke rose from a few of the fire pits, figures shifting in the practiced movement of the day's toil, of the cutting and cleaning and building that humans did by hand. I wondered still what the humans thought of Isa and her magic, but being so near the thrum of so many minds created a hardly bearable pounding and pressure in my head. *Taking precautions*, Junnie had said.

I didn't suppose it could hurt. I breathed a heavy sigh, wanting nothing more than to sit down somewhere far away from there or to sleep for what remained of the day, but there was work to be done, and once it was over, the journey back to our own beds.

"Eat," Junnie suggested.

I took a long swig of water and a hunk of bread. "Send something with us, and I vow I shall do so on the way home."

Her expression eased with her soft laugh. "Done. Do what you are able here, and I will watch over things so that you may finally rest." She squeezed my shoulder. "It's been hard-won and well deserved, my Freya."

I settled not on the barren side of the deadening, but on the lush grass of the fey lands, curling my ankles beneath my bent legs to lay the staff across my knees. Blisters burned beneath the salves and leaves Ruby had applied to my palm, but the bandage had not had time to fully set, so I scraped it free and wiped the salve on the soft grass. The exposed skin was red and torn, raw enough that just the sight of it made me feel ill. Chevelle settled beside me, and I curled my fingers closed.

"This can wait," he reminded me quietly.

"No," I said. "No more waiting. I want to go home."

Rhys and Rider approached, taking watch from the sparse trees nearby, should they be needed, and Ruby sat on my other side, picking blades of grass and lining them up in a pattern on her palm. I gave her a glance then wrapped my hands around two points of the staff. Chevelle lay his palm against me, and as I grasped tighter to that connection between us— our bond—fey figures began to shift from behind the trees.

High fey and lesser, beings of feather and flesh, of jutting bone and delicate wing, masters of ice and wind and fire, all watched and waited.

I closed my eyes, willing the energy within me to flow toward the stone mounted in the head of the staff. Through Chevelle, I felt the strange void that was the deadening, the darkness that was capable of stealing energy from the fey. Near the settlement it was not as powerful or as dangerous as what we'd just faced, but unlike before, in the settlement and beyond, it had been set free. It was not tied to a river of darkness but had flooded the land and was somehow spread by the human inhabitants.

Between the fey and barren grounds, I weaved my magic, dark energy and light, into a tighter barrier than the repair I'd made at Hollow Forest. I had time to do it correctly, time to leave a lasting border, a threshold to prevent the darkness from leeching more energy from the fey and their land. I felt eyes upon me, and farther out, the minds of wolves and the indistinct buzz of too many human minds. I felt Isa, the half-human girl, and I wondered if she could feel the brush of my mind as well.

When my eyes finally came open, task complete, a long line of elves watched from the barren ground. Junnie stood beside Steed, Anvil among the Council sentries, light and dark elves joined in a single cause, their postures mirrored by the fey. Isa moved to stand by Junnie, her wide emerald eyes and dark hair such a stark contrast to the golden glow of my great aunt. The girl reminded me, somehow, of my mother, and the thought made me cold.

Chevelle's hand slid from my back, and my gaze stole away from Junnie and the girl. As my Second helped me to standing, the watching fey shifted out of the trees. They stared at the elves beyond me and then the ground, seemingly unchanged. Two wood nymphs came forward, their slender fingers reaching out, tips green and pointed with claws. The nymphs passed Chevelle and me without acknowledgment to kneel in the low grass before the boundary. They began to hum a tune picked up by a few in the crowd as several random chirps and sharp barks sounded from high in the trees. Chevelle's breathing was steady beside me, but I knew he very much disliked the situation, not to mention the fey in general. I wanted to get my Seven out of there before the sun set on the cursed day.

Then Junnie moved forward, coming to stand before the two fey, each on their own side of the border. Between the three, quite suddenly sprang a soft green vine covered in thorns. It grew up, falling over to spread in a line, tangling with new shoots that burst from the earth with startling speed, each of them weaving, not unlike the braid of energies below them, to form a visible boundary between the fey and barren land—*human* land.

The vines grew thick and woody, a tall, prickling fence spreading from where we stood to far beyond what my eyes could see. Steed gave me a wary look over the burgeoning hedge, but I only shrugged. Surely, Junnie would be able to create a passage through both her magic and that of the fey.

Anvil muttered, likely words to that effect, and Junnie shook her head, not unkindly, before a massive gateway rose out of the thorns. The wood nymphs said something nasty but apparently obliged. I didn't blame them for not wanting a single human to be able to pass, given that their presence could suck the energy—the life—out of the fey, but certainly they understood that Junnie and her men would need access to what waited on the other side. Isa and the humans would have to be looked after.

The tangling passage came to rest, the arching gateway

blooming with a black flower that I presumed was the handi-work of the fey, and the wood nymphs rose to meet their brethren. Several of the watching fey flew forward, reaching out to touch and test the thorns. There was a shriek as one was punctured, blood dripping to the earth from its hands. Where its blood splattered the grass, more black blossoms sprung up, to the delighted cackles of the watching fey, who appreciated flowers from blood.

I met Chevelle's gaze. "Yes," I told him, answering his expression. "Time to go."

28

FREY

W<small>E JOURNEYED HOME, WASHED IN OUR OWN ROOMS WITH CLEAN</small> mountain water, rested in our own beds, and had begun to heal as best we could with the help of Ruby's ministrations. I had never been more grateful for a few days of peace.

Liana had sent word, not a missive by pixie but by Veil's own guard, that Veil was recovering as well. I wondered briefly what the changeling might have been up to but let it fall aside for greater concerns. The deadening had been stopped. The madness my grandfather had incited was over. It was time, again, to move forward. It was what we'd been fighting for all along.

Junnie had followed after us a few days later, having spent time with the new boundary to be certain everything held in place. She'd left me with assurances, with wishes that all would be well, and with the return of the wolves.

Finn and Keaton had spent much time at the boundary between fey and elven lands, their magic strong despite the bonds of their animal forms. Junnie explained that the transference had left them able to do more with the ancient magic that made up the previous boundary than with the powers that most elves carried presently. The way she'd said it had tripped me up in my exhausted state, and I'd not had enough sense about me to ask precisely what she meant. But I'd read the journals from Asher's study. I'd seen the book with the missing page.

Junnie thought it was a magic I was capable of. She thought it was something maybe she could do herself.

I shook my head, absently dabbing my quill into ink in the predawn light of my study as Ruby's hands worked through my hair. She made a brief noise of disgust at its utter disobedience then tossed her hands skyward before settling them onto her hips. "It will have to do."

I smiled at the scroll as I made another mark. "Thank you, Ruby. I'm certain you have more pressing duties to attend."

She leaned over to, ostensibly, blow on the ink, my list in plain view. "More pressing, yes. More difficult is arguable."

"What of the new recruits?"

She shrugged, sliding over to lean against the edge of my table. "Willa seems to have most of them in hand. I've been letting her rough them up a bit before she brings them to me. That girl was born to shape soldiers." I leaned back to look at her, and she waved my words away before I'd even begun. "I know, managing the living and all that. She'll be well-rounded, I assure you. Edan has her set up for some missions in Camber. She'll learn both sides of death and the law."

I chuckled at her promise. "Stay out of trouble yourself then, aye?"

Ruby's emerald eyes were clear and bright. "Unequivocally." She gave me a curt nod before turning to go.

I set my quill aside, glancing once more over the list. Ruby's mood had improved dramatically since Grey had been put back to full duty, and her progress with healing his skin was impressive. I doubted Grey would ever be fully restored, but what was left of the marks caused him no pain, and he did not seem to mind. "There are worse scars," he'd told me, "than those we wear on our skin."

Those scars, I understood all too well.

Anvil rapped a knuckle on the open wooden door, and I turned to face him. "You called for me?" he asked. His gaze did not scan my attire, though Anvil had been around long enough to know I only dressed as such when I had official castle duties to attend. I beckoned him in, and he settled into the chair across from me.

"I've asked so much of you over the years."

His expression cut me off, and in the silence, he said, "You've nay asked anything of me. It was always given of my own free will, and you well know it."

"Let me do something for you."

His dark gaze was as steady and calm as ever. "You've done all I could have wished for, young Freya. It has been my honor to serve you."

I leaned forward. "To serve at my *side*."

He leaned forward as well. "For the North. However you parse it."

"I was afraid you'd be difficult," I said with a smile.

Anvil chuckled, giving me a glimpse of the rare softness behind the giant of a man. I had known him since I was a child. Duty and honor were what drove him. He would not accept a gift for something he thought his responsibility.

"Time off, perhaps? Maybe a little journey into the wilds?"

His gaze narrowed on me "You thinking of capturing more beasties?"

I laughed and leaned back into my chair. "Anvil," I said, my tone quite plainly changing the subject, "I am grateful to have you, and the North owes you a debt. Call upon either when you see fit to claim your reward. Until then"—I slid the parchment from my table, handing it over to the most imposing of my Seven—"I entrust you with seeing out these tasks."

He took the document, glancing briefly at the list. "Aye," he said. "It would be my pleasure."

As he headed for the door, I called to him, "One more thing." When he glanced over his shoulder, I smiled. "Meet us in the stable when you're done."

~

I WALKED THE FAMILIAR CORRIDORS, a path I'd known for as long as I could remember, and resisted the urge to trail my fingers down the cool, dark stone walls. I was no longer a child running with Chevelle, chasing after him in play or as we attempted to evade my grandfather's guards, no longer the wild halfbreed girl who frightened the elders unreasonably. Those days were gone—lost, like so many other things, to the past. I was head of the castle, Lord of the North. And in my blood ran the magic of both the dark and light elves.

I had not wanted the responsibility of leading a kingdom, but my choices had been taken from me. I was grateful, for the first time in my life, that such had been done. I had the power to change things. I was going to right so many wrongs.

At the entrance to the throne room, my Second waited, striking in his official garb. I gave him a private smile, and he inclined his head, never taking his eyes off me. "Has everyone arrived?" I asked.

"As you requested."

"Excellent," I told him. "You know I love a good summit with the locals."

Chevelle barely held back a smile, as he plainly knew I

loved nothing of the sort. He gestured toward the passageway, allowing me to enter first.

I came into the throne room to find a dozen leaders from Camber and other Northern towns, as well as a few clan leaders and a half dozen representatives from the rogues. I did not sit but stood at the edge of the dais, looking down on the men and women whom Anvil and Chevelle had chosen. "I call you here today to bestow upon you a great responsibility."

The men and women before the dais shifted, duty and honor ideas they had more respect for than me, a half-human girl who'd been a catalyst for the massacre that had nearly destroyed their home.

"You have been chosen not for your fealty but for your worthiness of the post." I let my gaze trail the line, meeting with elves who'd known me since I was a child, who'd shown allegiance to my grandfather because they'd had no other choice. "I will not rule by games and by blood, but there are those who will challenge us—challenge my rule—with such." My palm was empty of its staff, the stiff bandages Ruby had placed over my wounds replaced with soft woven fabric and coated in salve. But my fingers were not curled into a fist. My anger was gone, acceptance in its place. Difficulties were what it was to rule. As Chevelle had once promised, we would face whatever came together.

"Now that things with the fey and with Council are settled, we shall put into place protections against future trials that may arise. A commission of leaders who are made aware of the workings of this kingdom and may react when—if—their lord is in peril." *Taken*, I meant. *Killed*. Any of the things the previous Council of light elves or my grandfather had tried to do.

"As such, I will not name my successor. In the event of my

death, a new lord will be elected by my Seven from a pool of candidates designated by you."

The gathered leaders fell still, their wary gazes frozen on me. I could see when their comprehension registered, when they realized that Asher's only remaining heir was the half-human girl who resided past the fey forests, the girl who they understood—now that rumor had spread—held no elven magic at all.

"Aye," said Dagan. At his word, the others startled, but Dagan's dark eyes never left mine. He nodded. "I accept your task as my duty and swear to fulfill it with all faithfulness, and should need be, my life." The rogue beside him scratched his beard, but Dagan took a knee. "I swear my fealty not merely to the North, but to you, Lord Freya and daughter of our blood. By my honor."

Beside him, Emiline also took a knee. "I, too, swear my fealty and pledge to serve with honor and—should it come to that—my life."

Bayrd was next, then Alianna. The rogues did not take a knee but pressed their hammers to their chests. "Aye. For the North."

And as the final present made his vow, the line of them echoed the chorus. "For the North."

～

WE STOOD in the courtyard in the waning light, Steed in his black guard-issue uniform, Chevelle and I across from him, still in our formal attire from our day's business in the throne room. I'd had the courtyard cleared to meet with Steed, and it was evident he understood the import of that. Or possibly, he'd heard of the gifts I'd bestowed upon the others.

"We do not perform our duties to be rewarded." Steed's

tone was earnest, his shoulders straight, his hands crossed behind his back. He looked good in the uniform, despite all the years he'd spent in battered leather and well-worn cloth.

"It does not lessen their impact," I told him. Then I smiled. "And it is not the last I will ask of you."

Steed chuckled, though I wondered if he'd any true idea. But that could wait.

"You were the hardest," I said. "Fortunately, I had help from your sister on that front."

Steed's smile fell, his dark eyes suddenly wary. At the change, Chevelle chuckled beside me.

"I suppose we've chaffed you enough." I glanced toward the shadows beneath the stone ledge at the edge of the courtyard and called, "Anvil." There was a shifting in the shadows, and then three dark shapes moved out of the darkness, the soft landing of hooves on forgiving soil and the shift of fabric the only sounds. I felt the fluttering brush of my heart against my ribs, the strangeness of animals who lived off the fey energy. I looked back to Steed. "There were so many creatures lost to the deadening. Before we knew anything of it, the fey and those who subsisted on that energy were falling prey to the darkness. Veil and the others did try to save what they could, but many were nearly wiped out."

Steed did not seem less confused by my explanation, but as Anvil and the others moved forward, their dark shapes became the clear outlines of two mares and a massive stallion. The animals wore long blankets draped over their backs, their manes falling over their eyes to taper off near fine-boned knees. Anvil held the stallion by rope and halter, but I had given the beast direction. He would not fight or run for the time being, at least. Behind Anvil and that stallion stood Barris with a mare, and beside them, Willa held another.

There would be more soon, as they were brought carefully over the boundaries in the cover of night.

"I've made an arrangement with the fey lord, Veil," I said. "In exchange for helping him bring back the creatures' numbers, the fey will provide a steady supply of fey energy, delivered within dragonstones."

Steed took his eyes from the horses, as if he was still not certain what the formality was about or why he would need such a supply of energy for horses.

I grinned full-out at him then gestured toward Anvil.

With a quick snap of his wrist, Anvil jerked the stallion's blanket free, and the beast leapt forward to shake his head and throw his massive storm-gray wings wide. The creature made Anvil look small, and when the winged breast whinnied, it cut through the courtyard in an absolutely chilling pitch. The flutter in my chest rose, but so did my grin.

Steed could not seem to look away. He stood slack-jawed and speechless at a creature the likes of which he would have never seen—never so much as expected to see.

Chevelle, watching the scene play out with a smirk, slid his hand across the small of my back. I leaned into his warmth, letting the comfort of our bond swell through me. It demanded nothing. I couldn't say that about much in my life.

I sighed deeply, overwhelmed with rightness and the feeling of *home*. But I had one more task to attend, and the light of day was nearly gone.

I straightened, drawing away from Chevelle and again into the posture of a proper lord. "We will leave you to it, Mr. Summit."

Steed turned to me, still apparently staggered by the shock of horses bearing wings, and blinked.

It took my best efforts not to laugh at him. "Should you

need assistance, Willa here has experience riding the creatures."

As I turned to go, I inclined my head toward the girl. It was the first time I'd seen her so pleased—she wore a bit of a feral grin. When we passed through the next courtyard, I could still hear the rumbling timbre of Anvil's laugh.

29

FREY

ANVIL DELIVERED THEA, THE LAST TO BE REWARDED FOR HER
part in procuring a dragon, to the doorway of my study with a
curt knock and an announcement that was far too official for
the smile playing across his lips. He'd witnessed enough that
day to know what I was about, and the idea apparently
delighted him. I bit my own smile back but acknowledged my
guard with the tip of my head. "Thank you, Anvil. That is all
I'll need for now."

As he turned, he gave Thea a little bump with his elbow,
forcing her either to lurch awkwardly or come fully into the
room. She chose the latter.

I stood to face her, still in full regalia, the length of my cape
nearly sweeping the floor but coming instead against the
blackened leather of my tall boots. "I've trusted you with a
great many things, Thea."

She stared at me with something like terror building
behind her deep mahogany eyes.

I did not let myself smile at her. Not yet. I stepped forward,
crossing the room to take her hand in mine. Her braid

181

appeared hastily done, but her uniform was intact. She wore three short blades at her hip, and one more graced her thigh. The last was carved wood, lightly etched with an intricate horse-head design.

I was not the only person who trusted the rugged girl from Camber who'd made good on becoming a guard. "You have not let me down," I continued. "Not once."

Thea swallowed hard, her mouth trembling with the apparent need to respond and what I guessed was the utter lack of any idea what to say. She couldn't know what was coming, only that I'd called her into my private study to discuss something of significant import. And she'd been delivered by one of the Seven before being abandoned to no one but me.

I released Thea's hand, crossing my own behind my back like a proper Lord of the North. "Thea of Camber, servant to the North, skilled healer, and trusted member of the castle guard, I hereby award you with a crucial charge, the first and sole of your order: Lord's Caretaker." She stared at me, obviously at a loss until I said, "It is your duty to oversee the care and protection of the first dragon of our great stable."

Her chin dug back before her words fell free. "I-I... Caretaker... for the *dragon?*"

After a moment in which she seemed to consider all that it might entail, and possibly running from the room, she glanced back at me, a dozen questions in her eyes.

I waited.

"I've no experience with dragons. I've no command of something that size. I can't imagine how—" She shook her head. "I am grateful for the honor, but I would much prefer something I can actually do. Like to care for the horses."

I bit back a grin at her tone. "I can appreciate that, truly, Thea. But this charge will require someone with skill. And not necessarily patience. I can think of no one else with the determination and fortitude required for a duty such as this." I did let myself smile then, gently, and could see that the gesture made it hard for her to argue.

"I'm destined to fail," she said quietly. "To let everyone down."

"It will be a learning endeavor for both you and the animal, but you will have a band of guards at your command and—should you need it—my assistance with the beasts. And Ruby, of course. She is fireproof, after all."

Thea stared at me, clearly overwhelmed, and I gave her a curt nod to indicate that I considered the matter resolved. She stared on as I walked past her, but just as I reached the open door, I heard her turn.

"Wait," she said, "what do you mean *beasts*?"

I glanced over my shoulder, giving her my best parting smile. "Perhaps you should meet with Rhys and Rider when they return. Study up a bit on how to manage a trove of dragons."

∾

I SLEPT FITFULLY THAT NIGHT, despite the feelings of warmth and rightness I'd experienced during the light of day. When I woke the next morning, I knew there was one last task before me, one final piece to settle my concerns.

Junnie had given me and my Seven the most precious gift —she'd offered unrestricted access to the Council libraries and her own personal cache. She'd given us the knowledge of the entirety of the light elves' collection. Rhys and Rider had left the same day I'd told them, only delaying long enough that they might arrive bearing fitting gifts for the gesture the new Council head had bestowed. But I understood it was not only to benefit the North. It was a gift that would help save us both.

It was a gift she feared we needed. Junnie had concerns of Isa, the girl who, despite never having known her mother or Asher, had been conceived with plans to be a great king. Asher had been wrong that the child would be male, but he had not been mistaken in the potential of the gift he'd cast upon her. Isa had the capacity to move countless humans, to bend them to her will. And any power so great could be a dangerous, deadly thing.

If we could not trust Isa, we would have to control her.

So at dawn, before the entirety of the castle had risen and before Thea had taken to caring for her new charge, I felt for the mind of my dragon. Isa was far from the castle, far from the eyes of any of her father's blood, and farther still from the reach of the light elves. She understood that the rule neither of Council, who would kill her, nor the North, who would count her as nothing despite that her father had been lord, could actually hold her there. The settlement and beyond was the only place she could truly be free. And beneath her, under her direction, were the countless humans and her guard of elves as well.

From the comfort of my room, I urged the dragon to flight, to abandon the warmth of its nest in the keep. It rose to stand, twisting its spiked neck in a lengthy stretch before shifting to the platform's edge. It wanted to roar into the hazy air but only rumbled out a groan at my behest to please not wake the entire kingdom. Then the beast shook free what little dew had settled on its scales and drew in a deep breath through its nose.

It leapt into the haze, diving past the castle walls, down the mountain, and into the warmth of a rising sun. The earth called to it in a slow, persistent way, a steady beat that was not the thrum of fey energy Ruby had described. There was nothing urgent about the dragon's connection to its magic, no desire to fill its stores.

At the boundary between lands, we swung north, skirting fey territory to soar high above the trees. From that height, it was easy to see the demarcation—not from the wall of vines created by Junnie and the fey, but from the lush, verdant flora against the nearly barren ground. The trees beyond fey lands were sparse and thin by comparison, the land open in patches of trodden grass. In the mind of the dragon, I did not feel the press of the humans, but it wasn't long before I could see the damage their presence had done.

Encampments dotted the landscape in an ugly brown rash, scarred with dark smears of cinder and ash. There were fire pits, gardens, and shelters constructed of chopped-down trees. So many humans. So much barren ground. My stomach turned at Veil's remembered words. *A plague,* he'd called it. *An infestation.*

The humans had been driven from lands farther out by the changelings. Asher's motives might have been lost to his death, but they were not incalculable. My grandfather had intended to rule all the lands, to reign over every kingdom within his reach through his children. I could only be grateful we'd stopped him, and I understood that we'd only done so by working as one. Our kingdoms had united to save us all. It was not a lesson any of us would soon forget.

The dragon soared closer to the settlement that was Isa's own small kingdom, the land she'd managed to turn into a village with herself at its head. The sun had risen fully, but the dragon had made good time. We would be able to beat even the spread of rumor at that rate, and my connection to the beast had not dwindled in the least. Back in my bed, my chest eased in a sigh at the realization, and I pressed the dragon toward the edge of the settlement, over the creek from which Junnie had diverted water toward the new boundary.

Our shadow rolled over turned earth, and I urged the dragon faster as I recognized the dark hair of my grandfather's child. She only looked up for a moment before we slammed to the earth, the dragon's talons tearing into the trodden soil of a well-used path as the villagers nearby started to scream. The girl looked up at us from where she stood alone on the path, her hair flipping back in the wind, her green eyes wide. She wore no cloak, but a sleeveless gilt-trimmed robe laced high up her neck, and her feet were bare. She stood very, very still.

The dragon purred out a breath, puffs of sulfurous smoke piping from its nostrils into the warm morning air. Behind her, Isa's sentries rushed forward, bows and staffs in hand. The humans ran for cover, apparently not under her direction to heed other commands. I let the dragon lean forward menacingly, eyes on Isa's own. The girl was no fool, and she would have heard the rumors. She would have known the beast was under my command. She held up a hand, and the sentries froze in their tracks, waiting.

The dragon's tongue flicked out, tasting the air. Isa flinched at the sight of its teeth, and I urged the dragon to pull its lips back into a terrifying smile. Isa took a steady breath then knelt before the beast on one knee, her gaze never leaving the dragon's. The beast watched her for a moment before it drew its head up, coming to its full height to stare down at the petite girl whom Asher would have made king.

The dragon raised its head skyward and let out an earsplitting roar that shook the barren ground beneath them. A stream of fire followed the sound, but it fell to nothing more than heat before it scorched the earth. It looked at Isa one last time with a warning before its gaze traveled her line of golden-haired sentries and the humans cowering in the trees.

Isa understood the power the elves possessed. She understood, more than that, the power I held on my own.

She knew what the dragon meant. She understood she would be under our rule. I urged the beast to turn, its massive wings going wide to nearly brush the ground, and with a single thrust, it launched again into the air to circle once over the settlement before heading back toward home.

~

I MET the dragon on the platform atop the keep, standing to greet him after his leisurely flight and a hasty meal. The beast did not seem reticent to share its desires, but when left alone to its devices, it had returned each day to the keep. I wasn't certain whether it was the ready supply of food and lack of anyone trying to kill it that called for its return or the companionship offered by those who resided within the castle. Ruby, I'd noticed, had left the creature quite a supply of energy-laden gems and jewels, not to mention a fragrant plant I'd not yet identified. It wouldn't be long, I supposed, before I caught her napping in its roost.

The dragon landed gracefully on the platform, shuffling nearer with care to see what I might have brought it. I laughed softly, opening my palm to show that it was empty of anything other than the offer of touch. It didn't seem to mind, lowering its snout toward me so that I could scratch between its scaly ridges. We stood so for a long while as the sun rose and shadows shifted, and then the beast sighed and turned, heading back for a mid-morning doze in its newly constructed nest.

A warm breeze brushed across my skin as I murmured my

goodbye to the dragon and turned to make my way down the castle steps. I froze as a shadow shifted behind a column, because it was not one cast by the morning sun. It was Veil, watching me.

He moved from behind the column, where he'd been apparently contemplating me with the dragon. The outline of the fey lord's wings was a bit off-kilter since the changeling's attack. As I approached him, his face came from the shadows and into view, the small quirk at the edge of his mouth comment enough on my cooing attentions toward the beast.

"I thought you never wanted to see me again." My voice was even, but I couldn't hold back the hint of a smirk.

"I stand by my words." His arms were crossed gingerly over his chest, a silken-paneled shirt covering what would certainly be a well-bandaged wound. It would be Liana's handiwork—Liana, who had yet to return.

"And yet, here you are." I stopped before him, a fair distance away, given that we had recently been near war.

"A fool to the end," he said, though Veil was too much of a fey lord to pull off self-deprecation. Even with the injuries he'd received from the changelings, he was glorious in the early sun. Yet he stood there, calling himself a fool.

I crossed my own arms, mirroring his posture. "At least it is an endeavor you will not face alone."

He chuckled, shifting uncomfortably at the move. I was surprised he'd managed to fly so far, but not entirely so, given that he had repeatedly made clear that he was eager to put the entire mess behind him and return his court to order. "I bring you a gift, Lord Freya of the Dark Elves' Kingdom and healer of the land."

I felt my expression slip in my surprise, though Veil's gifts had not always been pleasant.

"Payment," he said, "for a bargain well made." At the shift in my brow, he shook his head. "Distrust, after everything." He drew a small square of parchment from the pocket at his waist. "May you not need this for centuries more." He inclined his head as he handed it to me, coming straight again to flash me a smile. "And may I not see you or that cursed dragon on my lands for at least as long."

A laugh bubbled up before I could stop it, and at that, Veil dropped off the edge of the roof, his wings popping wide to catch the warm summer air.

I watched him fade into the distance before I unfolded the square of parchment. My gasp echoed through the haze, bouncing off ancient stone and block put in place ages before I'd been born. My fingers trembled as my eyes roamed the page, over the fine lines and worn ink that seemed entirely unreal but were in my hands regardless of how impossible that seemed.

Behind me, the dragon let out a contented groan.

EPILOGUE

THE FOLDED PARCHMENT RESTED INSIDE MY VEST POCKET FOR A season, close to my chest and carefully hidden. I had not told Chevelle of what the page held. I had not told anyone. I would make a copy soon and send it to Junnie.

Liana had not returned from fey lands, though we'd had word that Veil's court was well in order, with the changeling woman at his side. My only contact with the fey had been through court liaisons, those who'd brought missives or dragonstones or whatever minor business in which correspondence might be required. I couldn't say I missed it, even a little bit.

Late one evening, Ruby fetched us from dinner to the stables, where Steed had been watching over the mares Veil had sent. The horses subsided on fey energy, and like everything fey, they did not follow the rules of life outside the boundary. Summers were long on fey lands, and the horses could foal twice a year. We had not expected to see results so soon, not when the animals had been displaced. But the fey were resilient, and Steed was the best at what he did.

So my Seven gathered around the courtyard walls with myself, Thea, and Willa, who'd apparently taken my offhand comment to help Steed as order, to watch the first foal from the herd come into the world. Chevelle stood beside me, his palm warm on the small of my back. Ruby was at my other side, her fingers twined with Grey's. Thea stood on tiptoe, though she was tall enough to see over the wall, her hands pressed hard against the stone. She'd fallen into her duties as caretaker with far more ease than any of us expected, though I'd watched her at first to be certain she would be safe. The dragon had taken to her, no doubt in part to the herbs Ruby had urged Thea to tuck into her braids, and the two had seemed to work out any disagreements with little to no blood.

Steed had never seemed happier. I regarded him in the short grass of the courtyard, crouched low as he watched the mare take a final, groaning roll. Her wings were tucked tightly against her back, the lines of her body taut with pain. There was a distressed call from inside the stable, where the stallion was locked away, and then the tingle of magic rolled over the clearing as the mare screamed a reply.

The foal was born only minutes later, and in mere minutes more, it stood on wobbly legs. Its wings were wet and matted, its body an ungainly bundle of twigs. The foal was a mare, as black as night. It would take time for white hairs to sprout, for its gray coloring to come in, and more time for the babe to learn flight. But it was alive and hale, and it took two jaunty hops before crashing awkwardly to the ground.

Ruby covered her grin with a palm, and Anvil snorted a laugh. I glanced at my companions, my heart pressing hard against my chest, emotion swelling so that it felt as if I might not be able to contain it. The way Grey smiled at Ruby, the way Anvil bumped his elbow against young Willa, the way

Thea stared in awe of Steed and that foal... I had never been happier. I had never felt safer or less alone.

I had never expected anything of the sort.

"I have to tell you something," I whispered to Chevelle. I glanced up to find his eyes already on me—not on the foal, not on the others. I didn't have to ask what he'd seen there. I could feel it in every part of my being.

I pressed a hand to my heart then slid my fingers inside my vest. The parchment came free, and my lips crawled into a nervous smile as I passed the small square to Chevelle. His brow drew together, but he stayed close as he unfolded it carefully between us. No one was watching his face as he read. No one saw the understanding pass over his features but me.

I felt the breath rush out of him as his head came up. He stared in shock. Whether he was waiting for confirmation or explanation of where I'd gotten it, I didn't know. It didn't matter.

Veil had gifted us the missing page, which contained the key a powerful elf might need to shift, like the ancients Finn and Keaton, into a beast after their time on Earth was done. The key could allow us to carry on forever.

I looked at Chevelle, at what might have been tears welling in his deep blue eyes, and lifted a shoulder in a shrug. It was nothing I had ever expected.

I had never been happier.

Thank you for reading The Frey Saga. Check out a new epic fantasy adventure from Melissa Wright: *Seven Ways to Kill a King.*

SHE WAS BORN A
PRINCESS.
THEY MADE HER
AN ASSASSIN.

SEVEN WAYS
TO KILL A KING

She was born a princess. They made her an assassin.

One was an accident. Two a coincidence. By three, they would know. It would be harder, but I would avenge my mother's death. These kings would pay that price.

Seven cities make up the Storm Queen's Realm, each of their self-crowned, murderous kings are one of Princess Myrina's marks. The treasonous curs may have banded together to share a stolen throne, but soon they will fall.

They thought her dead, killed in the massacre. They thought their rule secure, but Myrina of Stormskeep has awoken. With

the help of her loyal bloodsworn, the shadow princess will
have her revenge.

*For fans of The Witcher and Game of Thrones—a new princess set
on vengeance is here to steal your heart.*

∾

Find it Now

∾

ALSO BY MELISSA WRIGHT

THE FREY SAGA

Frey

Pieces of Eight

Molly (a short story)

Rise of the Seven

Venom and Steel

Shadow and Stone

Feather and Bone

SEVEN WAYS TO KILL A KING

Seven Ways to Kill a King

DESCENDANTS SERIES

Bound by Prophecy

Shifting Fate

Reign of Shadows

SHATTERED REALMS

King of Ash and Bone

Queen of Iron and Blood

HAVENWOOD FALLS

Toil and Trouble

BAD MEDICINE

Blood & Brute & Ginger Root

~

Visit the author on the web at

www.melissa-wright.com

Lightning Source UK Ltd.
Milton Keynes UK
UKHW020641210922
409198UK00009B/901